The Power of Un

Nancy Etchemendy

AN
APPLE
PAPERBACK

SCHOLASTIC INC.

New York Toronto London Auckland Sydney
Mexico City New Delhi Hong Kong Buenos Aires

ISBN 0-439-31331-7

Copyright © 2000 by Nancy Etchemendy. All rights reserved.
Published by Scholastic Inc., 555 Broadway, New York, NY 10012,
by arrangement with Front Street/Cricket Books, Carus Publishing.
SCHOLASTIC, APPLE PAPERBACKS, and associated logos are
trademarks and/or registered trademarks of Scholastic Inc.

12 11 10 9 8 7   3 4 5 6/0

Printed in the U.S.A.   40

First Scholastic printing, November 2001

Interior designed by Ron McCutchan

For Max & Claire

With special thanks to
Lianna and Ray Bennett,
Nina Kiriki Hoffman,
the Tuesday Night
Writers, and my editor,
John Allen.
                    —N.E.

TABLE OF CONTENTS

The Power
of Un

STRANGER IN THE WOODS

Stories used to be easier to start before I found out about the innermost workings of the universe and all that stuff—I mean, back in the days, maybe a week ago, when I was just Gib Finney, a regular guy with a bedroom full of birds' nests, stringless yo-yos, baseballs, half-eaten Baby Ruths, and computer parts.

The Power of Un changed everything. Not just obvious stuff, like my leg, which is very broken because of it. That's the reason I'm lying here in a cast on a cot in the backyard, staring up at the autumn stars. The Power of Un also changed everything I thought I knew about the world. Big things, like what's good and what's bad and what lies ahead of me. Little things, too. For example, before all this, I never would have wondered if my whole future depends on whether I slurp up this marshmallow that's floating in my cocoa. Sometimes it just about drives me crazy.

Because of the Power of Un, I realize this story has about a million possible beginnings. Maybe it started a year ago, when my little sister, Roxy, went on a class trip to the animal shelter and became obsessed with dogs. Or maybe it began the day my best friend, Ash Jensen, and I saw a carnival poster in the window of my mom and uncle's hardware store and we swore on a dead sparrow that we'd go no matter what. But I guess the clearest place to start is with that spitball I shot at my math teacher, Ms. Shripnole, known among her students as Ol' Shrapnel.

That stupid spitball changed my life. Who knew? Not me. Not at the time, anyway.

But in order to understand the true meaning of the spitball incident, you first have to know what happened between me and Rainy Frogner earlier that fateful Friday.

On the morning in question—October 27— Lorraine Frogner and I sat practically nose to nose, whisper-shouting at each other in the science lab at Mitchell Rutherford Middle School. I have no idea why Mr. Maynard assigned us both to the same table. I'd never been able to hide my irritation with Rainy Frogner, though I sometimes wished I could. It often made me look like an idiot, and who wants to look like an idiot?

I'm not sure why she had this effect on me. In spite of her unfortunate name, Rainy Frogner has her good points. She's smart, for example, and she's generous. She's lent me lunch money more than once. And she isn't exactly ugly. In fact, she's pretty easy to look at. She has this really unusual combination of shiny black hair and mint-green eyes. Still, I'd often catch myself thinking of her as the most pestiferous girl on the planet. I got into arguments with her all the time, and when I tried to figure out why, I could seldom find an exact reason.

That day, though, I *did* have a good and exact reason for arguing with her. She was on the verge of ruining our science experiment. We were supposed to do a lab project with potato skins, and we could take our choice: dunk them in water, pour ammonia on them, blow-dry them, dip them in lemon juice, or figure out something original. Since original stuff is my idea of serious fun, I convinced Rainy we ought to pour salt on our potato skins.

I had a pretty good idea what would happen. I've watched my dad salt potatoes in a pan before he fries them. He makes a mean hash brown, and he says one of the keys is not to salt them too much at first, because if you do, the salt will draw out all the water, and you end up poaching them instead of frying them. Salt does that—draws the water out of stuff. Like when you put it on slugs, which I've only done once, and it made me puke. But I'm getting off track.

Rainy thought we ought to pile the skins in a mound and lightly salt them—like she wanted to keep from making a mess or something. She's kind of obsessed with neatness and with doing things *correctly,* which, I guess, are two of the things that bother me about her. I thought we should spread the skins out, then really pour on the salt. Experiments in which hardly anything happens are boring, and I was hoping for big results.

"Come on," I said. "If it gets messy, I'll clean it up."

Rainy's reaction shocked me. She said, "Gib Finney, you are so bossy and mean! Why does everybody always have to do things your way?"

"What are you talking about?" I said.

"We're already using salt, just because *you* wanted to. You're so selfish! You never think about what somebody else might want."

"I am *not* selfish! I just want a good experiment. We should use plenty of salt because if we don't, nothing'll happen."

Like I said, we were whisper-shouting at each other by that time. I didn't like being called selfish. My face was getting hot—I really wanted to yell or throw something, and it was taking a lot of effort not to.

Then Rainy said, "O.K. Have it your way." She

picked up the box of salt, opened it all the way, and turned it upside down. The potato skins got covered, all right. So did everything else, including my lap and the floor. There was no way to tell what was happening to the skins, so the experiment was useless anyway. And I had to spend a lot of time under the table with a whisk broom and a dustpan. On top of it all, Mr. Maynard gave us points off for horseplay. By the time the bell rang, I was having a hard time thinking about anything except Lorraine Frogner's head exploding. Which is probably why I did what I did (or more accurately, didn't do what I didn't do) during the Spitball Incident later that day.

We have math with Ms. Shripnole every afternoon at two o'clock. I wish we had it in the morning, because you have to concentrate in order to do math. By two everybody, including Ol' Shrapnel, is tired and wants to be someplace else. On Friday afternoons it's the worst.

The classroom was a little too warm, because it was an Indian summer day and the sun was pouring through the windows. Ash and I pretended we were working on decimals, but to keep each other awake, we passed notes back and forth, making plans for the carnival that night.

I opened my binder to get a fresh piece of paper, and a forgotten soda straw fell out. I like to keep straws around; they're good for so many different things. Stick them in a glass of water and make volcano sound effects. Blow bubbles with the hand soap from the bathroom dispensers. Scare flies. The possibilities are endless. But what I love most about them is that anytime you need a little excitement, you can shoot things out of them. Like spitballs.

Ash hid a grin behind his hand as he watched me take a fat, juicy wad of paper and load it into the straw. I had no idea that, seated in the desk on my right, Rainy Frogner was doing the same thing, with me as her target. Spitballs aren't something Rainy generally does. She hardly ever gets in trouble, but now she was risking it for the second time that day. She must have been pretty mad at me.

I waited till Ms. Shripnole turned around to write something on the board. Then I took careful aim, blew out that big, wet glob with all the force in my lungs, and hid the straw as fast as I could. My plan was to hit her in the back. It would stick there, all the kids would laugh, and she'd have no idea why. It wasn't the most admirable thing I've ever done. It definitely wasn't the smartest thing I've ever done, either. Believe me, I spent a lot of time regretting it later.

In the course of a split second, two unexpected things happened. First, I felt something cold and wet hit my cheek with a lot of force. It was Rainy's spitball, and it stung. Then mine hit Ol' Shrapnel.

Unfortunately, she'd just turned around at the worst possible instant, and it hit her directly in the forehead.

The whole class gasped as if it were a single organism. Before any of us could take another breath, Ms. Shripnole's face went through a series of contortions, beginning with surprise and ending with fury.

"Who did that?" she demanded, casting her gaze around the room like a laser beam.

To my considerable surprise, the laser came to rest not on me but on Rainy, who was still holding the straw she'd shot me with. It all took such a short time, I doubt anybody in the room had a clear idea what had happened except Rainy and me and maybe Ash.

"Lorraine Frogner!" said Ol' Shrapnel in a tone that would have made even the principal shiver.

"But . . . but I didn't do it. Gib did it!" Rainy waved her straw in the air while she made this claim.

"Lorraine, it is bad enough to do such a thing in the first place, but to deny it under these circumstances is far worse."

I could have stopped the whole scene at that point just by standing up and admitting I was the one who'd shot the offending spitball. It would have been the right thing to do. But I was angry. I'd spent a chunk of the morning on my hands and knees under a lab table. And I could still feel the cold sting of Rainy's spitball on my cheek. So I squinted at her and sat still. I let her take the blame for what I'd done, thereby sealing my fate.

Have you ever watched a spider walk across a web on a misty morning? It might only step on one tiny strand of silk, but the whole web moves. Then far on the other side, a dewdrop might fall and jiggle other strands of silk or maybe even break one. The whole shape of the web can change because of that one eensy step.

That spitball was a spider step. It was just one little thing, but it made other things happen, one after another, till the whole shape of my life was different. And not in a good way, either.

Ash had a soccer game after school that day, so our plan was to meet at his house after dinner, then walk over to the carnival. We had a lot of ideas about what to do once we got there—play the games, get lost in the House of Mirrors, eat way too much junk food. We'd heard that the fortuneteller, Madam Isis, was spookily great. And we wanted to ride the rides, of course. There was a new one we'd never been on called the Devil's Elevator, and it was supposed to be pretty good. Jeffrey Hargrove said it made his big sister barf, which was an outstanding recommendation.

After school I went home, dumped my books, and said hi to my dad, who usually comes home around three from work at his rare books store. Then I did a bunch of stuff just to kill time till dinner. I played "doggy" with Roxy, which I hardly ever do. Who in his right mind wants to pretend his kid sister is a dog?

It's bad enough if you have to take a real dog for walks, feed it, and brush it. Doing those things to a dog-obsessed six-year-old is totally weird. But I was in a good mood, so I said yes when she asked me. After that I shot some hoops above the garage door. When I came back inside, my dad was on the phone, looking serious.

"Oh, don't worry," he said. "These things happen. Gib can take care of Roxy. Hope you feel better soon."

He hung up, and I could see from his face that he was about to tell me something he knew I'd hate. "That was Lorraine Frogner," he said.

At first I wondered what Rainy was doing on the phone with my father. Would she seriously complain to my parents about the spitball thing? Then I remembered she was baby-sitting Roxy that night because Mom and Dad were going out and so was I. My stomach did a somersault and ended up somewhere around my vocal chords.

"She can't baby-sit?" I croaked.

Dad nodded. "She says she's not feeling well. Sorry, kiddo. You're going to have to watch Roxy tonight."

"N-Not feeling well? She was fine at school today. I don't get it." But even as the words were leaving my mouth, I got it, all right. Rainy wasn't sick. She was mad and she was getting even with me.

"Some kind of stomach bug," said Dad.

"But I'm going to the carnival tonight! Ash and I have been planning this for weeks!"

"Well, you can take Roxy with you. I know she'd love to go."

"Take Roxy?" A pain was growing somewhere behind my eyes. A picture formed in my brain of me going on the baby rides, holding Roxy's hand—which would be stuck to mine with cotton candy—and taking her to the Porta-Potties. "Dad! If I do that I won't have any fun at all! Can't you guys just . . . I dunno . . . skip the dance tonight or something?"

He and Mom were going with my aunt and uncle to a square dance, one of those dumb things where everyone dresses up in Western clothes and stomps and whoops for hours while a country band plays songs with names like "Flop-Eared Mule" and "Shindig in the Barn." I couldn't imagine why anybody would want to do such a thing.

"Look, we don't want to cancel our plans any more than you want to cancel yours," said Dad. "Of course you'll have fun. You'll just have Roxy along while you're at it."

"But, Dad . . ." By now my voice was barely a squeak.

"No buts." I knew by the way he said this that further arguments would just make things worse. Besides, I was afraid I might start crying.

The room was beginning to feel incredibly small

and hot. I opened the front door. "I'm going for a walk."

"Make sure you're back in time for dinner," said Dad. His voice trailed after me as I closed the door. "Sorry things worked out this way. . . ."

Sorry. *Sure,* I thought. There was an empty Coke can on the sidewalk in front of our house, and I kicked it as hard as I could. Then I found a rock, and I kicked that, too, every time I took a step, all the way to the woods at the end of the block. I wished I were an only child, that Roxy had been kidnapped from the hospital at birth or had been bitten by a tropical mosquito and died of malaria before the age of two. I wished Lorraine Frogner knew the meaning of the word *mercy.* Most of all, I wished I'd never heard of spitballs.

There's a path through the woods, and I started to run along it, still kicking everything I came across. Dry leaves flew up in fountains. Twigs sailed through the air. The last thing I kicked was a tree trunk, and it hurt so much I had to sit on the ground, holding my foot and saying every swear word I knew.

I was pretty distracted, so it came as a shock when I looked up and saw, through a blur of angry tears, someone standing just a few feet away, watching me. I probably would have yelped if I could have, but I was so startled my throat closed and I jumped up, ready to run, before I had time to think about it. There was such a roar of rushing blood in my ears that I could hardly hear anything else, and the world seemed eerily quiet.

Whoever it was stood in the deep shadow of a tree. The sun was about to set, and the woods felt too dark for comfort. The figure wore a long, shapeless garment—maybe a trench coat, maybe some kind of robe. When he opened his mouth, he spoke in a deep, raspy voice. "Don't be afraid. I won't hurt you."

He might as well have said he was an ax murderer. He took a step forward, and there was just one word in my mind, flashing like a neon sign: RUN. Unfortunately, the heel of my high top caught on a root as I tried to back up. I landed hard on my rear.

The old man loomed over me. He smelled strange—like hot metal or lightning. I thought I saw smoke rising from his rumpled clothes and a wild halo of silvery hair that stood out from his head. He had an object I couldn't identify in his raised hand.

"I've got something for you," he said, and he opened his mouth in a crazy grin.

THE GIFT

The old man continued to smile at me, his head tilted. Anybody would have thought he was admiring a famous painting or something. I squirmed. I'd never seen him before in my life—he could have been the premier of Siberia for all I knew. There was no way he could have something for me, at least not anything good.

"Wh-Who are you?" I asked. Not that I expected an answer. I was stalling for time while I felt around on the ground for a rock or a stick—anything I could use to defend myself.

He took another step forward, and I got a better look at his face; shining eyes set in woven creases of skin. I could see the rest of him better, too. His coat—or robe or whatever—looked soft and crumpled.

Maybe he'd slept in it. From certain angles, it glittered, and there really did seem to be smoke or vapor rising from it. Maybe he was homeless, but even so, I'd never seen anyone like him. He was clean, but that electrical smell was very strong. I wondered if he'd escaped from a mental hospital. Anything seemed possible.

"Who am I? Not important," he said. "Not important at all." He laid one finger beside his mouth and frowned. "Well, that's not quite right. It *is* important. It's important that you not know. It's also important that we hurry. I don't have much time."

My fingers closed around a nice, thick stick in the fallen leaves. I grabbed it and raised it over my head. "Get away! I'm warning you."

His eyebrows drew together. He held up the hand with nothing in it, palm toward me as if to shield himself, which made me feel a little braver. "No, no, don't worry. I'd never hurt you. Cross my heart and hope to die." He traced a cross over his heart. I wasn't sure I'd ever seen anybody older than thirteen do that before. "I'm just here to give you something. Really," he continued, holding out his other hand. What I'd assumed must be a gun or a knife or some other weapon was actually a flat box that looked like it might be plastic. In the dusky light, it was hard to tell.

One of my mother's favorite warnings scuttled through my skull, and I said it aloud before I could stop myself: "Beware of strangers bearing gifts."

The old man closed his eyes for a second or two and smiled. When he opened them again, he said, "This is so weird. So great and weird." He looked . . . well . . . *delighted* is the only way I can describe it.

I sat up. *Great* and *weird?* These weren't words I expected to hear from a guy who had to be at least seventy. My heart finally slowed a little, maybe because he seemed to find all this just as strange as I did.

"Your mom's right, of course. You shouldn't take gifts from strangers," he said. "At least not under normal circumstances."

My heart sped up again. How did he know my *mother* had given me that warning?

"But these aren't normal circumstances. Far from it!" He laughed, and I surprised myself by lowering the stick. It was the kind of laugh I've heard from my dad when he finds a rare book in perfect condition. Ash laughed that way once after we took a clock apart and put it back together and it started ticking. It wasn't the laugh of an ax murderer.

The old man held the box up so I could see it better. It was about the size of a paperback book and looked a little like an overgrown calculator or an electronic game, but not quite like either one. The case was gunmetal gray. It had a keypad and colored buttons that might have lit up.

He reached toward me. "Let me help you up," he said. I thought about it for a second or two, then took his hand, which felt firm and cool. Not strong exactly, but solid. I dropped the stick in the leaves and brushed myself off.

"You kind of startled me a little," I said.

"Couldn't help it. It's unavoidable. I tend to appear suddenly." He glanced at his wrist. So did I. He wasn't wearing a watch there, but a small, square panel gleamed in the skin on the back of his hand. Maybe it was some kind of watch after all, because he said, "I tend to disappear suddenly, too. Sorry to rush you, but I really have to hurry. There's no way of knowing how long it will be before the . . . well, there's no word for it yet . . . before *things* begin to deteriorate."

The guy was beginning to sound weird again, and I licked my lips, looking around for my big stick. But before I could bend to retrieve it, he said, "Isn't there a good place to sit somewhere near here? We need to talk." His voice was cheerful, and by this time I did want to ask him roughly a gazillion questions. So I decided to forget about the stick.

There's a big, flat-topped rock in the woods where I sometimes go to think or just be alone. It was where I'd been headed when I left the house, so I led him there. It wasn't far, maybe fifty or sixty feet down the path, but he walked slowly. He had a bad limp and he was wearing these funny little slippers, so thin they must have felt almost like no shoes at all. Along the way, he talked nonstop.

"How are things at home?" he asked.

I felt like saying not so hot, but I wasn't sure how much I wanted him to know, so I just said, "Oh, I dunno."

"How's Doofus?" he asked with a strange, soft little smile.

"Doofus?" I frowned, partly because his nosiness was starting to annoy me, partly because the question and the way he asked it were so completely strange. Maybe he had me mixed up with somebody else, and this whole thing was just one big mistake. "Who's Doofus?"

He made a sound like "phhtt" and rubbed his forehead hard. "Silly me," he said, waving a hand in the air as if swishing away gnats.

When we came to the rock, he sat down on it with a sigh. Walking the short distance seemed to tire him out. He patted a place beside him, inviting me to join him.

He looked at the back of his hand again and frowned. "We'd better hurry," he repeated. He lifted the little box so we could both see it better in the twilight. "This is yours. It's what I came to do, give you this." He spoke very fast, the words tripping over each other so I had to listen hard. "This is important. Remember what I'm telling you. This is a device, a delicate piece of equipment. As you can see, it's hand-made. It's the only one of its kind."

Now that I had a better look, I could see he was right. It reminded me of a found-object sculpture. There was a little screen at the top, maybe an LCD. But it was slightly crooked. So were the number keys below it. There was a large red key that said **ORDER** in bold letters. The little buttons that might have been lights were different sizes and colors, as if somebody had stuck together whatever was handy. They, too, sat crookedly in the face of the device. A strip of battered black tape held the front of the case to the back. The whole thing looked like a piece of junk.

"Are you positive you've got the right person?" I asked. By now I was really beginning to wonder. Nothing about this made sense.

"Your name is Gibson Finney, right? And you live at 410 Cherrywood Drive?"

"Yeah, that's me."

"You're the right person, then. There's really no doubt."

"But I don't understand."

The old man sighed through his nose and smiled. "That's what I'm trying to do. Help you understand. Now, please listen carefully, because we're running out of time, and I still have a lot to explain." He was beginning to remind me of a teacher. "I want to ask you a question," he said. "Have you ever made a mistake in a game and asked your opponent if you could take your turn over again? Say, a bad move in checkers, or you were unfairly distracted while trying to shoot a basket?"

"Sure. A do-over," I said. "Everybody needs a do-over sometimes."

"You can do this with your computer, too, am I right? If you make a mistake, there's an 'undo' command. Give it, and you're back where you started before you made the error."

"Sure, it's one of best things about computers."

The old man's eyes shone. "Exactly! And what if you had a machine that gave you the power to undo any mistake? Not just in a game, but anytime, anywhere, any mistake at all?"

"Wha—" I said. His meaning hit me all at once, so hard I couldn't finish the word. I could barely even finish a thought, there were suddenly so many of them jostling each other in my brain. "You mean, this machine . . . I could . . . with this? . . ."

"Yes," he said. And he flashed a huge grin.

My heart was galloping again. I reached for the box, then stopped myself. "Could I touch it?"

"Of course. It's yours." And he started to give it to me. I reached out for it, but an inch from the little machine, my hand stopped as if there were invisible bricks in the air. I pushed hard. I could see the old man was pushing, too. He clenched his teeth. Veins in his arms and neck stood out. "Come on," he whispered. "This has to be possible!"

He grunted and shoved so hard he almost fell off the rock when my hand finally touched the box.

It was heavier than I'd expected and cool against my skin. I stared at the screen and the keypad in the dusk and wondered if I was dreaming. Everything that had happened since I met this strange old guy was unbelievable.

"Are you serious?" I asked. "Undo any mistake? A chance to do anything I want over again?"

"Well, there are limits, of course. But basically, yes, do anything you want over again. We call it the Power of Un."

"Why me?" I whispered.

The old man looked at me in that strange way again, as if I were a piece of art in a museum or some other weird thing. He smiled, but he never answered the question. Instead, he went on as if I'd never asked it. "Shall I explain how the unner works?"

Unner. The word sounded magical. I said it softly as I looked at the controls and realized they made no sense at all. I recognized the letters and numbers on the machine, but they were arranged in mysterious ways. There were letters beside the screen: **H**, **M**, and **S**. And there were words, if you could call them that, under each of the three colored buttons: HMODE, under a round yellow one; MMODE, under a bigger blue one; SMODE, under a square greenish button that looked as if it needed to be straightened. The numbers 1 to 9 were arranged on the keypad, but there was no 0. Then there was the big red **ORDER** button. *Order what?*

"Yeah, how does it work?" I asked.

There was a sudden movement in the shadows not far off. The old man turned sharply toward it and said, "Not yet, I need more time! Can't you get me just another minute or two?"

I stared in the same direction but couldn't see anything, though I heard a faint hiss that rose and fell like voices on a bad phone. A chill scurried up my spine. "What's going on?"

The old man stood up slowly, as if he didn't really want to, and began to back away from me, shaking his head. "Ironic. I've run out of time! I'm sorry, Gib. Believe me, I'd stay longer if I could. We're just not very good at this yet. I'll be gone in a few seconds, whether I want to go or not. You're going to have to finish learning about the unner on your own. It won't be easy, but I know you can do it."

The shadows were so deep and he had moved so far from me that I could barely see him. "Wait! I have no clue how to work this thing," I called.

He was all but invisible, but his disembodied voice, fuzzy and echoing, floated through the evening woods. "Sorry about the zero. I was in a hurry. No time. Take it with you tonight. But Gib, watch out . . ."

"Watch out for what?" I ran toward his voice, but he disappeared into the gloom.

The pumpkin-orange light of a rising hunter's moon peeked between tree trunks. A chilly breeze rattled the dead leaves that hadn't yet fallen. Somewhere nearby an animal I couldn't identify made a chittering sound, and I shivered, my hand sweating on the greatest power any human being, living or dead, had ever held.

FEAR OF THE DARK

I went back to the big rock and sat down. Fix any mistake. Get a second chance at anything. Ideas poured into my head, one on top of another: flunk a test, take it over again; swing at the ball as many times as I wanted till I finally hit the winning home run; make bets with people, and if I lost, go back and bet the other way. This was better than winning the lottery!

My hands shook as I studied the unner in the twilight, turning it over and over, brushing the keypad with my fingers, touching the screen. It took me a minute to get up the courage to press one of the keys—the 9, because I've always liked that number.

Nothing happened.

No numbers appeared on the screen. No lights lit up. The little box made no sounds, ominous or otherwise.

I pressed a bunch of different keys. Nothing. I pressed the colored buttons. Nothing. After a while I got so desperate I even squeezed my eyes shut and dared to punch the **ORDER** key. Still nothing. Maybe the old man was just a crazy vagrant after all, and the amazing machine was no more than what it seemed: a cobbled-up pile of junk that had never worked in the first place.

Deep twilight had crept into the woods, and I could no longer see things clearly, not even my own hands on the unner. Luckily, my watch has a tiny, built-in light. A quick look confirmed what I already feared. I was late for dinner. My parents are fairly reasonable about a lot of things, but *late for dinner* isn't one of them. If I didn't get home soon, there was a major possibility they would ground me. In which case, abandon all hope—the carnival might as well be on Mars.

I jumped up from the rock and started to run back along the path toward the house. There was no daylight left anymore, just the faint glow of moonlight wherever it could find its way between the branches. Confusing checkerboards of shadow dappled the ground. I thought I knew every inch of that path and could have run it blindfolded, but I was wrong. The toe of my shoe caught on something—I couldn't tell what it was—and I sprawled facedown.

I turned over and sat up, spitting leaves, and rubbed the tip of my nose, which burned. I'd scraped it on something. I forgot about that completely, though, when I realized the unner was no longer in my hands. I peered around but couldn't see it anywhere in the chaos of leaf shadows.

Stay cool, I told myself. *You'll find it.* But my stomach didn't believe me. It felt suspended in midair, as if I were falling out of a tree. Still on hands and knees, I crawled all over the forest floor, scattering leaves and dirt like a maniac.

I spent five precious minutes searching, knowing that every lost second moved me closer to being grounded. Finally I had to admit it was useless. I needed light. So I headed reluctantly for the house again, mumbling the worst words I could think of.

By the time I ran up the walk, Mom was standing at the front door with her hands on her hips. A ruffly square-dance skirt mushroomed around her waist. I never would have told her so, but it looked all wrong on her. I'm used to seeing her in the clothes she wears at the hardware store: canvas carpenter pants and a green shirt with her name on it. The best plumbers in town listen with respect when she talks about the difference between copper and galvanized steel. Whenever she wears those frou-frou square-dance ruffles, it's like looking at a kid's puzzle: What's Wrong with this Picture?

"Gibson Finney, where have you been?" she said. She never calls me *Gibson* except when she's mad. And she never calls me *Gibson Finney* unless she's really, *really* mad.

"Over in the woods, kicking rocks and, I dunno . . . thinking," I said. Realizing how lame that must sound, I added, "I would have been home sooner, but there was this weird old guy in there and he . . . wanted to talk. Sorry." I knew a second later that admitting I'd been talking to a stranger might not be the best way to convince her I shouldn't be grounded. I stared at my shoes and tried to get myself ready for whatever would come next.

"I ought to ground you! You were talking to a stranger? A man? In the woods at night?" She made it sound as if I'd decided to shake hands with a crocodile.

"Well . . . I only said a couple of things. He did most of the talking."

Then I felt her hands on my cheeks, which surprised me more than a little. Her eyes still had sparklers of anger in them, but when she spoke, her voice was softer than before. "You had me so worried, honey. Are you all right?"

I smiled a little. We'd moved from *Gibson Finney* to *honey*. Maybe there was hope after all.

Then she noticed the scrape. "Oh, your poor nose! Did he hurt you? If he hurt you I'll . . . I'll make him wish he'd never been born, that . . . that . . ." She patted my arms and shoulders semihysterically, maybe checking for broken bones. Her cheeks were bright red.

I felt strangely happy. She would actually make somebody sorry they were ever born if they hurt me? She sounded like she meant it.

"Mom, Mom, it's O.K. I was in a hurry to get home and I tripped in the woods. That's all." I stopped her hand just as she started patting my hips. "He didn't touch me. He didn't even *try* to touch me. He was just a crazy old homeless guy or something. All he did was talk awhile. Then he disappeared." I didn't mention the unner, though I felt a little guilty about it. Something inside me wanted to keep it a secret, at least for now.

She frowned and touched my face beside my nose, almost on the scrape but not quite. The wound was probably dirty, and I suppose she was battling to keep herself from brushing at it. She may be unusual in some ways, but when it comes to obsessively cleaning open wounds, she's the same as every other mom in the known universe.

"You're sure he didn't hurt you?" she asked.

"Positive."

She looked doubtful for a second, then pulled me firmly toward the house. "Well, let's get that scrape cleaned up. Your dinner's ready. Roxy's already eating, and Dad and I are leaving in a minute."

Before long, I had a Band-Aid on my nose and was seated beside Roxy at the table, shoveling down a big helping of Dad's beef stew.

"Do you think we should call the police?" Mom asked Dad as he helped her don a mind–numbing jacket with fringe and sequins.

"Mo-o-o-m!" I said. "He didn't *do* anything. He just talked to me."

"There's nothing so bad about that," said Dad.

"Yeah, but anybody who hangs out in the woods at night is creepy," said Roxy. "I'm scared!" She held her butter knife with both hands, as if she might have to use it for self-defense.

"He wasn't creepy. And he's not hanging out! He's gone. I already told you," I said.

Mom frowned as she picked up her purse—which had fringe like her jacket, plus red, white, and blue stars and stripes. I squirmed when I realized I was glad I wouldn't have to be seen with her.

"What if you only *think* he's gone?" she asked. "He could still be out there, hiding. What if he watched you walk home and he knows where you live . . ."

Dad said, "Sh!" and gave Mom a fierce look. "Gib, are you scared?"

"No!" I didn't want to get the old guy in trouble. I was beginning to feel sorry I'd ever mentioned him.

Dad shrugged and held his hands out, palms up. "There's your answer. Gib's not scared. I trust his judgment. Rox, you don't need to be scared, either. Gib's got the situation under control."

Roxy frowned and huffed.

"Oh, all right," said Mom, sounding annoyed. She kissed me on the cheek. "But you be careful, Gib. You and Ash and Roxy stick together at the carnival. Don't dawdle. And," she gave Roxy a kiss, too, "have a wonderful time."

I couldn't help rolling my eyes a little. Dad grinned at me as soon as Mom wasn't looking, and they waved as they closed the door behind them.

I peeled the Band-Aid off my nose and looked at the clock on the wall. I was supposed to meet Ash at 7:00. It was already 6:45, and Ash didn't know about the Roxy debacle yet. I needed to make another change in the plan, too. I wanted to get a flashlight and look for the unner before we started for the carnival. I figured I'd better phone him as soon as I finished dinner. I grabbed a hunk of bread and used it to soak up the last of my stew.

"Roxy, hurry up and finish. It's almost time to go," I said with my mouth full.

Roxy crossed her arms and slouched in her chair. She'd hardly eaten anything. "I don't wanna go," she said.

"Wha-a-t?" I stopped with a piece of bread halfway between the table and my face. If it wasn't one thing, it was another. I was beginning to think this might be the worst day of my life. "What's the matter now? You love the carnival. It's going to be lots of fun!"

"No it won't. You and Ash'll make me go on the scary rides."

I sighed. That settled one question. We were going to spend the night on the baby rides. "No we won't," I said.

"Promise?"

"Promise."

"Cross your heart and hope to die, stick a needle in your eye?"

"All right, already! I promise. Cross my heart and hope to die."

She smiled, picked up her spoon, and started eating.

While she finished dinner, I phoned Ash and broke the news to him. He wasn't happy, but what could he do? It was either put up with Roxy or go to the carnival by himself. He agreed to meet us at the edge of the woods.

I got my baseball jacket and a sweater for Roxy. Then I grabbed a flashlight and a house key from the kitchen drawer, took Roxy by the hand, and locked up behind us.

The farther we got from the friendly glow of the porch light, the tighter Roxy held on to me. "How come we're meeting Ash by the woods instead of at his house?" she said in a small, shaky voice.

"I just want to spend a few minutes looking for something I dropped there this afternoon," I said. "It's perfectly safe."

"Nuh-uh! What about that creepy guy? What if he gets us?"

I gave her hand a little tug. My patience was getting threadbare. "Will you stop being such a worrywart? First of all, that guy wasn't creepy. He was actually kind of nice. And second, he's not there anymore!"

As the woods came into sight, she said, "I wish we had a dog. A big dog, like Old Yeller or Lassie. With big, fat teeth. A dog that'd scare that creepy guy so bad he'd have to wear diapers."

I almost laughed. "Don't worry," I said. "I'm bigger than Lassie." I did my imitation of a growling, barking dog, and Roxy giggled, which I took as a good sign.

When we got to the woods, Ash wasn't there yet. I told Roxy she could either wait for him out by the street or come with me into the woods. Instead of answering, she started to cry and latched on to my jacket with both hands.

"Will you please stop being such a scaredy-cat? There's nothing here now that isn't here in the daytime."

"How do *you* know?" she said.

I rolled my eyes again and gave up trying to reason with her. I took a step toward the dark trees—or, to be more accurate, I *tried* to take a step. Roxy clung to my jacket like a forty-pound monkey and screamed as loudly as she could.

"Cripes!" I said. "Be quiet! Everybody in town can hear you."

"I don't like this place," she wailed. "I wanna get out of here."

"Roxy, how am I supposed to do anything? You're

such a little dork!" I probably should have been more patient with her, but so many things had gone wrong since that morning, I felt crabby at the whole world.

Roxy switched from screams to pitiful moans. "How come you're being so mean to me? You . . . you dumb meanball!" She scrubbed at her eyes. Her hands had stew on them, because I'd forgotten to clean her up after dinner. "Ow! *Owowow,* I got something in my eye, it hurts, it hurts . . ." she howled. "I hate it here! I wanna go home!"

I felt like kicking trees again. First Rainy Frogner, now Roxy. How come girls always thought I was mean?

"Look, I'm sorry I called you a dork, O.K.? Don't cry." I tugged some of my T-shirt out from under my jacket and used it to brush her face off. "Is that better?"

Before she could answer, we heard the crackle of leaves under something's footsteps. Roxy's spine-freezing scream sliced the darkness like a knife.

MADAM ISIS

I grabbed Roxy and covered her mouth as the nearby woods came alive with the scuttlings and flutterings of unseen creatures. My own heart banged against my ribs. There's nothing like the sound of pure terror to get your blood fizzing with adrenaline.

"Who's there?" I said, trying hard to keep my voice steady.

"Gib? It's just me. Ash!"

I let the breath out of my lungs in a long, deep rush. It wasn't all relief. Some of it was embarrassment. My flashlight beam came to rest on Ash's familiar freckled face and well-worn Giants baseball cap. He was laughing.

"Hey, it's not funny, all right?" I said. "You shouldn't sneak up on people in the dark." Then, realizing how wimpy that sounded, I went on in a hurry, "I mean, not me. Little kids like Roxy. You could give her nightmares doing that kind of stuff."

"Sorry. I didn't think I was being *that* scary." He clamped his hands over his mouth to muffle a laugh. He could hide the smile on his mouth, but he couldn't hide it on the other parts of his face. It kept sneaking out and making his eyes squinch up and his eyebrows go crazy.

Ash's frantic efforts to control himself were so funny—and Roxy and I were so glad he wasn't a bear, a ghost, or a serial killer—that pretty soon all three of us were laughing.

"Oh, man, I'm really sorry," he said, catching his breath at last. "But anyway, I'm here now, so let's get going. Carnival ahead!" He turned, ready to lead the way up the street, but I stopped him.

"Wait a second. Um . . . first would you mind if we take a quick look for something I dropped in the woods this afternoon?"

"Are you serious?"

I nodded.

"Aw, Gib, come on! Every minute we spend here is a minute we lose at the carnival. What could be so important?"

"Yeah!" said Roxy.

I shrugged, aware that anything I told Ash I would also be telling Roxy, and I'd never known her to keep a secret. Not even the time I promised her a whole bag of Jelly Bellies not to tell Mom and Dad I had four live cockroaches in a jar under my bed.

A pained frown replaced Ash's smile. "You'll never find anything in the dark in all those leaves. Unless it's tickets to go on the next space shuttle or something, it's a waste of time to try. Come on. I'll help you look in the morning."

"Yeah!" Roxy said again, still looking scared. "Let's get outta here."

If the unner could really do what the old man said, it was *better* than tickets to go on the next space shuttle. Part of me worried that it might get stepped on or carried off by animals if we left it lying in the woods all night. But some other part of me knew it wasn't safe to let myself believe in the unner yet. After all, I hadn't been able to make it work when I'd tried it earlier. It would be pretty embarrassing if I delayed us for something that turned out to be a handful of useless junk. Besides, I, too, was anxious to get to the carnival.

Ash waved his fingers in front of my eyes like a hypnotist. "Think about it: cotton candy, rides, hot dogs, Madam Isis tells your fortune. I see in your future a big prize at the coin-toss booth!"

"Yeah! Yeah!" cried Roxy, jumping up and down with her hands clasped under her chin. "Could you win me a stuffed dog? Please, please, please?"

I shook my head and managed a tiny smile. Dad says a good sport always smiles in defeat.

So the three of us headed for Lafferty Park and the carnival a few blocks away. The chilly autumn air carried the faint screams of people on the Tilt-a-Whirl, or maybe the Devil's Elevator, rising and falling like waves. And every now and then a whiff of popcorn and roasted peanuts beckoned. They filled me with such anticipation that the old man and the unner began to fade from my thoughts. In my excitement, I even stopped caring about Rainy Frogner and her effort to spoil things. I was headed for a carnival with Ash Jensen, and it was going to take more than a dumb, vengeful girl, more than an annoying kid sister, more than a lost dream machine, to keep me from having a good time!

Soon we drifted happily among moving lights, clowns on stilts, and the guys with tattooed arms who ran the rides and the booths. We'd been saving up for weeks, and Mom and Dad had given me extra money for Roxy, so we bought a whole bunch of tickets for games and rides. Roxy wanted us to go straight to the coin toss, where a big blue-and-brown stuffed animal that might have been a dog gazed down balefully on the players. But Ash and I had other ideas. We went to the Freaks of Nature show and filed slowly past glass jars where two-headed lambs, spiders the size of dinner plates, and the brain of a genius floated in colored liquids. Then we went to the House of Illusions, which made us feel as if we were giants or mice or couldn't stand up straight. Roxy said it made her feel like barfing, so we got her a lemon-lime soda, Mom's favorite medicine for upset stomachs.

While she drank it and Ash and I decided what we wanted to do next, a flea-bitten brown dog ran past. It wasn't any particular type of dog, just a mutt whose fur ranged from scruffy to completely absent. Its ribs showed, and it had no collar. Roxy shrieked, "Poor doggy!" She dropped her drink on the ground and ran after the stray, looking totally delighted.

It took us five minutes to catch up with her. The dog kept scooting under tables and behind counters, weaving its way in and out of off-limits areas. Roxy was small and agile enough to follow it almost anywhere. Every time we thought we had her, she disappeared between somebody's feet. A carny with big muscles and a cigar grabbed her by the collar just as she was about to dart into the machinery of the Ferris wheel. The dog threaded its way through to the other side and disappeared before anybody could catch it.

Roxy cried and swung her fists, a long way from connecting with any part of the carny, while he held her at arm's length.

"Leave me alone, you big bully! You made me lose my dog!"

He looked at us sourly and said, "This yours?"

We nodded.

"Well, keep hold of her, or all three of you are outta here. We can't have kids running around in the machinery. Good way to lose a body part." He pushed Roxy in our direction with a snaggle-toothed leer. If he was trying to scare the living daylights out of us, it worked.

I grabbed Roxy's hand, and we ran away as fast as we could. We didn't stop until we reached the midway.

"Roxy!" I said. "You know better than that. Don't ever run off again."

"But I have to help that doggy!" She was already swiveling her head around, looking for the stray, and I knew if she saw it she'd run after it again without a second thought.

I put my hands on either side of her face and forced her to look at me.

"Hey! Lemme go!" she said, wiggling.

"Listen to me! Don't ever run away like that again, you hear me? If you do, I'll tell Mom and Dad, and you'll be in big, *big* trouble." I tried to keep my voice down but I couldn't quite manage it.

She twisted out of my grasp and stamped her foot on the dusty ground. "Tattletale, tattletale! You're not the boss of me! I can help a dog if I want to."

A tide of something hot as fire rushed through my blood. I couldn't remember ever being so angry before.

It was the whole thing—the fact that she was here at all, ruining my plans and Ash's; that she was being such a gigantic pain; that she was calling me names on top of it. At that moment, if there'd been any way for me to become an only child, I would have done it. I wanted to get back at her any way I could.

I shouted, "You think I'm an idiot or something? Why don't you just say what you mean? You want to take that stupid mutt home. Well, you can't. Mom and Dad don't want a dog. You're never gonna have one, so just forget it!" All of this was true. They just hadn't told her yet.

Tears started in Roxy's eyes. "That's a lie! Take it back, take it back!" She leaped at me, her small fists flying.

Too mad to think about what I was doing, I got ready to give her a shove. It's a good thing Ash was there.

He touched my shoulder lightly. He was smiling, and the lights of the carnival danced in his eyes. "Look where we are!" he said. "Madam Isis!" It was almost a whisper.

"Huh?"

He gave me a little punch in the arm and pointed. At first the look on his face made me wonder if he'd found a twenty-dollar bill on the ground or something. Roxy and I both gazed along the line of his straightened finger toward a small tent just a few steps away. It was draped in purple-and-yellow satin. The sign on the front said, "Fortunes Told. Learn Your Future. Madam Isis Knows All. (Five tickets)."

Roxy tried to sound it out. "For-toon-us . . . what does it say?"

"It's a fortuneteller," said Ash. "Hey, you could ask her if you're ever going to get a dog."

"Can she tell me? Really?" Roxy looked enthralled, her anger forgotten. My own was evaporating fast, too. Madam Isis was one of the things I'd been looking forward to most. Kids at school who'd seen her said she was *really* good. Not that I believed in fortunetellers, exactly. I'd never heard one say anything I regarded as proof positive of strange powers, though I confess I hoped I would. Mostly I just loved the shivery atmosphere they created.

We ducked into the tent. Inside there was so little light that at first we couldn't see anything at all. From some distant corner, a soft tinkle of wind chimes floated, even though the air was deathly still. A strange scent hung invisible before us, so thick I wondered whether I could touch it if I reached out. Madam Isis's tent smelled like smoke and spice, with a very faint undercurrent of something else: lightning. I was sure of it. It was the same smell that had surrounded the old man in the woods!

As our eyes adjusted, the outlines of the fortuneteller emerged from the darkness. She was sitting very straight with one hand to her heart as if we'd surprised her, though I knew that couldn't be the case. Why should she be surprised to see customers? I squinted, trying to see if steam or vapor was rising from her clothing as it had from the old man's. But there didn't seem to be any.

Ash eagerly handed over five tickets. Madam Isis, her face hidden in the shadows of a velvet cloak and long, crow-black hair, moved clawlike hands above a crystal ball. Her nails were long, and each finger had a tiny tattoo of an Egyptian scarab on it. I'd never seen a fortuneteller this convincing before.

She looked up at Ash. I caught the gleam of greenish light in a dark eye. "I see you flying." Her voice was rough as canvas, and she had a foreign accent. "No . . . not flying. Floating. In a small, bright place within a huge darkness." She stared into the ball. "Wait. Not darkness—a sky filled with stars."

"A spaceship?" said Ash. I could hear the awe in his voice. For as long as I'd known him, he'd dreamed of becoming an astronaut.

Roxy pushed in front of him, holding her tickets out eagerly. "My turn! I want to know if I'm getting a dog."

Madam Isis gave Roxy a long look that I knew meant something, though I wasn't sure what. She seemed worried or sad or maybe a little of each. She bent over the crystal ball once more, her scarab fingers circling the air above it.

"It's difficult," she said. She wiped the ball with the generous sleeve of her dark gown, then moved her face closer to it. After a few seconds she stared straight into Roxy's eyes and said, "Yes, I see you with a dog."

Roxy jumped up and down, squealing, "Yes! Yes! Yes!"

"But there is more, child. Listen to me. This is very important." Something in her voice stopped Roxy cold. Madam Isis seemed almost to have forgotten about her crystal ball. While she pinned Roxy with her intense stare, I finally got a glimpse of her face. It wasn't what I expected. She didn't look haughty or mysterious. She looked kind and a little tired, like somebody's grandmother. But that wasn't all. Her eyes shimmered with what might have been held-back tears.

Ash saw them, too. "What's the matter?" he asked in a hushed voice.

Madam Isis showed no sign of having heard him. Her whole attention seemed focused on Roxy. "You will only get this dog if you are very, very good tonight. You must stay with your brother and his friend. You will see a dog, but you must not run after it. Not under any circumstances. If you ever want to have a dog, you must not run after the stray tonight. Do you understand?"

Roxy nodded solemnly.

My mouth dropped open. How did she know I was Roxy's brother and Ash was just a friend? How did she know about the stray? Had she been spying on us earlier, or . . . I hardly dared to think it . . . did she really have supernatural powers?

"Very well," said Madam Isis.

Before I could even say *awesome,* Roxy became her usual self again. "I'm getting a dog! See, Gib? You were *so* wrong. Dog! Dog! Dog! Dog!" she shouted. She looked like she was riding an invisible pogo stick as she propelled herself toward the tent flap.

The fortuneteller frowned at Ash and made a scooting motion with her hands. "Go after her, boy," she commanded. "Don't let her out of your sight. You can't imagine how important it is."

Ash raised an eyebrow. I could see he wasn't ready to leave. I could also see that Madam Isis had spooked him. She had definitely spooked *me.*

Ash shook his head and ducked out after Roxy. I started to follow, but Madam Isis said, "Gib," and touched my hand. A thrill ran through me like electricity. Maybe it was just the shock of hearing her say my name, but at that moment I felt certain of her power.

"H-How do you know my name?"

Madam Isis pressed her fingertips together and touched them to her lips while she contemplated me in silence. Finally she said, "I have been visited by a messenger, an old man. Where he is from, who sent him, and why, I cannot tell you. All I will say is that he did not seem entirely of this world. He appeared in an instant, as spirits often will, and he left the same way. He described you, your friend, and your sister perfectly. He told me your name. He said that a terrible crossroads lies before you tonight—a moment when you will make a decision that may have terrible consequences. His warning to you is this: He sees a dog. He sees your sister running after it. If you let her, all is lost."

I swallowed hard, my throat desert-dry. She could only be talking about the old guy from the woods! I didn't understand, though. Roxy had already run after the dog, and nothing awful had happened as far as I could tell.

"That doesn't make sense. . . ." I began.

But she held up a finger for silence. "I can say no more, except be very careful. This is a dangerous night."

Then, fast as a cat, she rose, whirled, and disappeared through the back of the tent.

"Madam Isis!" I called after her. But she was gone. I didn't see exactly where she went. Maybe there was an exit flap hidden in the shadows. Maybe not. I was left alone with the jingle of wind chimes and shivers running up and down my backbone.

I bent and squinted into the crystal ball, but I saw nothing. Nothing at all.

VIEW FROM THE
DEVIL'S ELEVATOR

I raced out of the tent and looked around frantically. There was no sign of Madam Isis, but it was impossible to miss Ash and Roxy. Ash wobbled down the midway, a snow cone balanced on his nose, while Roxy skipped around him shrieking with laughter.

"Good trick!" she cried, clapping her hands.

As soon as Ash saw me, he said, "Whew! Thought you'd never get here." He handed the snow cone to Roxy, and we wandered down the midway while she licked it with ferocious concentration and I told Ash what Madam Isis had said.

"The funny thing is, I met an old man in the woods this afternoon," I said. "Now Madam Isis, who I don't even know, tells me he told her my name and gave her a message for me. And the message is all about Roxy running after that crazy stray dog. Something very weird is going on."

Ash chewed gently at the inside of his cheek, which he only does when he's thinking hard. "Not necessarily," he said. "Maybe the old man works for the carnival, too. Maybe he spies for her. Most people who claim to be psychics work with partners, you know. A spy could have heard me say your name. And a spy could have seen that whole thing with Roxy and the dog. That mean carny who said she was about to lose a body part, he was probably in on it, too."

"But how did the old guy know I was going to be in the woods this afternoon? He knew way too much about me, Ash, I mean it."

Ash shrugged. "Maybe he was spying on you all afternoon."

I thought about that for a while. I didn't want to believe him—I wanted Madam Isis and the strange old man and especially the unner to be genuine, not just a cheesy carnival act. And I hated the idea that somebody might have been watching me in secret. But I had to admit Ash had made some good points. "How could she know you want to be an astronaut?" I asked.

"How many guys do you know who haven't thought about being an astronaut at least once?"

I nodded, feeling defeated. He was right.

Neither of us talked much for a while after that. I let Roxy drag us along through the current of excitement on the midway while I thought about what a big disappointment the whole day had been. Eventually Roxy wheedled me into trying to win the bloated blue-and-brown stuffed doglike creature at the coin-toss booth. I threw quarters like a zombie, completely unable to keep my mind on what I was doing, until I realized I'd spent four dollars and had nothing to show for it.

"You can't quit now! You didn't win the big dog yet. You said you'd win it for me," said Roxy, sticking her lower lip out.

"I said I'd try. So I tried and I couldn't do it, O.K.?"

She made a scrunchy face. I could see she was getting ready to cry. Ash saw it, too.

"Hey, Roxy, why don't we try the carousel?" he said. "Look. You can pick an animal to ride. We can all go. It'll be fun."

From where we stood, we could see the carousel brightly lit and whirling. Horses, leopards, pigs, and elephants dipped and rose; brass poles flashed. A calliope waltz floated through the night air. "Could I ride a dog?" asked Roxy.

Ash grinned like someone with a slight stomach-ache. "Well, let's see if we can find one."

We didn't see a dog, though there was a wolf. That was close enough for Roxy. Afterward we took her to the kiddie-car ride, then the ponies. I stood guard while

Ash rode the Tilt-a-Whirl. Then he did the same for me. It was better than nothing, but nowhere near the fun it would have been together. Meanwhile I couldn't help turning to watch the Devil's Elevator every time a new crop of riders took the plunge. A metal cage carried them slowly up a tall, thin tower decked with lights. When they got to the top, the cage dropped like a rock, stopping fast in just the last few feet. More than anything else I could think of, I wanted to ride it. Not by myself— with Ash. It seemed like a small enough thing after such an awful day. There had to be a way we could manage it.

Near the pony ride stood a trailer cart where a woman with a lot of makeup was selling cotton candy, peanuts, and candy apples. I knew Roxy loved candy apples. She waited all year for them, because they were hard to find except in the few days before Halloween. Inspiration went off in my head like a party popper.

"Rox, you want a candy apple?" I said as the pony man lifted her down from the saddle.

"Yeah! Yeah! Candy apple!" she cried.

"O.K., I'll get you one. But you have to promise something first."

"What?"

"You have to promise you'll stand right where I tell you and not move even one inch while Ash and I ride the Devil's Elevator."

As I said these words, I felt an uncomfortable little prickling in the back of my neck. Madam Isis had told us not to let Roxy out of our sight. But then I shook myself, feeling silly. Madam Isis couldn't be for real. Besides, I'd watched Roxy all night, and nothing dangerous had happened. I deserved a little fun.

Roxy looked suspicious. "Are you tricking me? Am I gonna have to ride with you?"

"No. You don't have to. And you get a candy apple. As long as you promise to stay right where I tell you till Ash and I are done."

"Can I eat it while I'm standing there?"

"No problem. Deal?"

She smiled, said, "O.K.!" and joyfully stuck her tongue out through the gap where she'd lost her second front tooth the week before.

So we bought a candy apple and stationed her at the foot of the Devil's Elevator. "Remember, don't move even one inch," I said as I gave her the apple.

"O.K.," she replied.

Ash and I handed the last of our tickets over and climbed into the "elevator car," a metal mesh cage with benches and seat belts. Six people could fit inside, packed like pickles in a jar. We were loaded in with a bunch of girls who started screaming before the ride even started.

I could see Roxy through the mesh. Without front teeth, she was having trouble biting the candy apple, a problem I hadn't thought of. But she was still exactly where we'd told her to stand.

The cage jerked and began moving with a grinding noise. My heart sped up. The last piece of Madam Isis's warning flashed into my head with awful clarity. *Be very careful. This is a dangerous night.* What if she wasn't talking about Roxy and the dog? What if there was something wrong with the machinery? It occurred to me that I might be about to die. I pressed my nose to the mesh so I could see better. As far as I could tell, the machinery looked all right. But who could say for certain? One loose bolt could make a big difference.

Looking down, I saw Roxy stamp her foot in frustration and throw the candy apple in the dirt. She crossed her arms and scowled up at me.

"Stay put! You promised!" I yelled, partly because I really wanted her to stay where I could see her, partly because it felt better to be angry than to be scared spitless at the possibility of dying on this rickety ride. My blood thundered in my ears. It was impossible to tell whether Roxy had heard my shout above the crowd noise, the music, and the jingling racket of the ride motor.

Things might have been O.K. anyway if the mangy stray dog hadn't suddenly reappeared. It trotted straight to Roxy's discarded candy apple, picked it up in its mouth, and ran.

The cage had risen nearly to the top of the tower now. But even so, I clearly heard Roxy's squeal. "Hey, doggy, that's mine!" Maybe she was just happy to see the dog again, or maybe she really was angry that it took her apple. Whatever the reason, she forgot her promise and ran after it, her small feet raising dust clouds with each step.

I yelled as loudly as I could, first at Roxy to stop, then at the ride operator to let me off. I grabbed the mesh and shook it to get the carny's attention, but all I managed to do was make the girls in the cage with us shriek even louder. Ash shouted, "Gib, what's the matter?"

All I could do was scream Roxy's name over and over as I watched the scene unfold from our bird's-eye view and realized with sickening certainty that Madam Isis and the old man in the woods were way, way more than a slick carnival act.

The stray dog bounded full tilt toward the street, where dozens of cars and trucks sped past in both directions. Just a few feet behind, headed straight for disaster with her arms outstretched, ran Roxy.

My voice failed as the dog darted off the curb into the sea of zooming traffic. The sound of shrieking brakes cut through the din of the carnival. The dog kept running, miraculously untouched, and so did Roxy, but not for long. Someone on the sidewalk reached out to stop her, but she slipped through his arms almost as if he wasn't there at all. He put his hands over his mouth as he watched, powerless, and I thought with a jolt that he looked like the old man from the woods. Everything seemed to move in slow motion as I watched the bumper of a pickup truck get closer and closer and finally connect with my sister's fragile body. I remembered the tears in Madam Isis's eyes when she looked up from the crystal ball.

The sound of my own scream seemed faraway as the Devil's Elevator began its long plummet back to earth.

When I think back on it now, I have trouble picturing the rest of that awful night very clearly. It's kind of a blur—probably just as well. I remember the lights and the sirens and people holding me back so I couldn't see Roxy. I remember looking around for the old man, finding no sign of him, wondering if I'd just seen someone a little like him or if I'd imagined seeing him altogether. They wouldn't let me ride in the ambulance, and they wouldn't tell me how Roxy was, except to say she'd be fine, which I didn't believe. Two policemen delivered Ash and me to Ash's house. It seemed to happen without my doing anything at all except let myself be guided along. One of the policemen knew Ash's parents, it turned out, and he had a long talk with them, which I couldn't hear very well, because I was in the bathroom feeling like I might throw up.

I didn't want to hear what they said anyway. I was afraid they might be telling Ash's parents it was all my fault. Mom and Dad had trusted me to keep Roxy safe, and I'd messed up. I'd left her alone even though I knew I shouldn't. Worst of all, I'd done it for a completely selfish reason—five minutes on a ride that turned out to be stupid anyway. Now Roxy might be dead.

My fault, all of it.

When the policemen left, Ash's dad said he'd walk me home and stay with me till my parents arrived. I remember Ash stood in the doorway as we left, crumpling and uncrumpling his baseball cap in hands that just wouldn't stay still, looking as if it took all his strength not to cry. "Bye, Gib. See you tomorrow," was all he said.

On the way over, I asked Mr. Jensen if he knew how Roxy was. He squeezed my shoulder and said they didn't know yet, but the doctors were working hard, and they were very good at their jobs. I liked him for telling the truth when a white lie would have been easier.

The house was cold and full of dark places. Everything seemed wrong and different, transformed in the space of that one instant when Roxy met the truck. It was ten o'clock. I should have been tucking her into bed and reading her a story. Instead, she wasn't there, and maybe she never would be again. It was strange to realize that I gladly would have played doggy till doomsday if that could have brought her back in all her old healthy, annoying glory.

I was glad Ash's dad was with me, cheerfully turning on lights, starting a fire in the fireplace, and asking me if I'd like a cup of cocoa or tea. He was his same old tall, familiar self. He even smelled the same as always—like smoke, because of the stinky wood stove the Jensens heated their house with. I guess it was just good to know that at least one thing hadn't changed. I asked him to make chamomile tea, even though I don't like it that much. It's what Peter Rabbit's mom gave him after his big hassle with Mr. McGregor, and it seemed to make him feel so much better. I thought it might work for me, too.

My brain seemed out of whack in a way that's hard to describe. I felt cold and shaky and I couldn't keep my mind on anything for very long. I was incredibly tired, yet wide-awake at the same time. Mr. Jensen said it was because I was in shock, which I didn't believe at first. I thought you had to be hurt in order to go into shock. But Mr. Jensen said no, it could also happen from seeing something awful. Like my sister getting run over by a truck.

He wrapped a quilt around me and sat me down in front of the fire with my tea, which helped the shivering a little. But my brain still wouldn't work straight. For a second or two I'd think, *What am I doing here? I should be in the woods looking for the unner so I can erase this whole awful thing.* And I'd start to get up, full of certainty. Then I'd think, *I'll just rest a minute first. I'm so tired.* And I'd sit back down. Then while I was sitting there, I'd start to feel desperate and wonder if maybe I just dreamed up the old man and the unner because I couldn't face what I'd done to Roxy. Then I'd think that couldn't be right, because why would I have dreamed it all up before Roxy's accident even happened? And I'd remember the smell of lightning in Madam Isis's tent and the old man's message. The unner was out there, just lying in the leaves, waiting for me to find it and make everything better again. So I'd start to get up, but my legs felt heavy and wobbly, and I'd think, *I'll just rest a minute,* and the whole stupid thing would begin all over again.

At some point I must have fallen asleep without realizing it. I woke up and found I was lying in bed, window-shaped moonlight spilling across the blanket and my bare arm. Mom sat beside me, running her hand through my hair like she does when I'm really sick, saying, "Sh, sh."

"I didn't say anything," I said, only it came out more like, "I-n'tshee-ing." I couldn't seem to get my tongue to work.

A tear spilled down Mom's cheek, and she swiped it away. She was still wearing her square-dance jacket. The silvery moonlight made the sequins glitter like magic, and I fell asleep again, back into a repeating dream of trying to get up to search for the unner.

THE BIG RED BUTTON

When I woke up the next morning, the tired wobblies were gone. I lay in bed for a minute, picturing a horrendous scene in which I wandered out to the kitchen and asked Mom and Dad how Roxy was. I was afraid of what the answer might be, afraid of having to tell them it was my fault. I smelled waffles and bacon, usually my favorite breakfast. But I didn't feel very hungry. What I did feel was an overpowering urge to run to the woods and find the unner so I could undo the whole terrible mess.

I threw back the covers, pulled on some jeans and a sweatshirt, and headed for the front door. I had my hand on the knob when Mom called from the kitchen. "Gib, are you up? We need to talk."

I whacked myself on the forehead—I should've

been walking more quietly. "Could I just do one thing first? It's really important."

Mom came to the kitchen door holding a bacon fork. She looked pretty bad. Her eyes were puffy and had dark circles under them.

"This is really important, too. It's about . . . Roxy."

My throat got hot and dry all of a sudden. I could see the news wasn't good.

I was trembling by the time I sat down at the table. There was a place set for Dad—a yellow plate and a blue checkered napkin, a tall glass of orange juice, shiny silverware, and the newspaper still folded and unread. He wasn't there.

"Where's Dad?" I asked.

Mom took a breath but didn't say anything. She looked as if she might start crying any second. I felt my heart pounding slowly somewhere around my throat. The bacon continued to sizzle in the pan, just as if this were any other Saturday morning, but my stomach felt like a black hole. I couldn't stand it anymore.

"What?" I said. "If she's dead, just tell me, O.K.?"

"Oh, honey," said Mom. The bacon fork clattered to the counter as she hugged me and gave me a kiss on top of my head. "No, she's not dead. Dad's been at the hospital with her all night. He's still there."

She pulled out Dad's chair and sat down. She looked at me hard, the corners of her mouth drooping as if they were heavy. Maybe she was trying to figure out whether I was strong enough to hear what she had to say next, or maybe she was working up her own courage. "I love you, so I'm not going to lie to you. Her head is injured. She's got brain damage, and she's in a coma. Do you know what that means?"

I nodded. "She's asleep, but she can't wake up?" My voice came out thin and tight as a wire.

Mom nodded. "The doctors don't know what'll happen. She might wake up and be O.K. eventually. She might not. We just don't know."

About a hundred questions jammed my head at once. Before I could make the first one into a sentence, the phone rang. Mom jumped as if she'd heard a firecracker. She raced across the room and picked up the receiver before the second ring.

She said hello, and then, "The scans look bad? But what . . ." She listened for a long moment, then said in a voice that didn't sound like hers at all, "How can they know that? How can they be sure she'll never wake up?" And she started to cry. Only it wasn't just ordinary crying. It was much worse. It wasn't a scream. A scream would have been normal compared to this. It was like all the world's grief and sadness wrapped up in a ball you could hear and feel but not see.

I didn't know the details, but I knew enough. Roxy's heart might beat for days; it might beat for years. But she'd never talk, never move from her bed, never again be the person she was last night.

It's hard to describe how it felt knowing all this. I hadn't thought I liked her all that much. I'd mainly seen her as a set of problems to get around: keep her out of my bedroom, play games with her when I didn't want to, let her tag along with me even when I was doing things she was too little to do. Sometimes when she was mad at me, she lied to get me in trouble. "*Da-a-a-d,* I think Gib's about to hit me," she'd say, even when I wasn't. And when Dad scolded me for it, half the time she'd stick her tongue out just to make me even madder.

But knowing she'd spend the rest of her life in a coma changed everything. I thought about all the stuff I'd never do again. Never play doggy with her. Never defend her from bullies at school. Never feel big and brave letting her hide her face in my shoulder when we watched a scary movie together. She'd never have another candy apple or plate of Dad's beef stew. She'd never find out what it felt like to be a grownup. Her dream of having a dog would never come true. It was all my fault.

I don't know how much time passed while I thought all this. Probably not more than a minute, though it felt much longer. Suddenly I thought I'd go crazy if I sat on that kitchen chair one more second. I couldn't stand it. Everything was coming apart. I had to try something, even if it didn't work, to make things better again.

The unner.

I could have used it the previous night if I hadn't been such an idiot and dropped it in the first place. Then Mom wouldn't be standing here with tears spilling down her face, and Roxy would be O.K. *Take it with you tonight, but watch out,* the old man had said. He must have known this was about to happen. I didn't know how or why, but he'd come to deliver the unner to me, to give me a way of undoing the worst mistake of my life.

I jumped up and ran for the front door. "I'll be back really soon, Mom," I yelled. If she heard me, she didn't show any sign of it. She seemed to be standing in our kitchen with the phone dangling from her wrist, but she wasn't really there. The real Mom was someplace far away, down deep inside herself. I've never had a nightmare that scared me any worse than seeing her like that.

I ran down our front walk, angry at myself and angry at everything in general. It should have been stormy, black and rainy. But it wasn't. Birds chirped, and the sun shone down from a sky as pure as a blue crayon. It was as if the world didn't care one bit what had happened to Roxy. Where our walkway met Cherrywood Drive, I stopped short. There sat the mangy stray dog looking up at me with its tongue out and its ears up, its tail wagging just a little, as if it thought tail-wagging might get it in trouble.

It was right.

My breath came in ragged, shallow gasps. I felt hot and sad and furious. Of all the places in town that stupid dog could have gone to beg for a handout, it had to choose my house.

"I wish that truck had hit *you!*" I cried. I picked up a pebble and threw it with all my might. I don't know exactly what made me aim wide. Maybe it was the way the dog sat, its head tilted, trusting me even though it shouldn't have. The pebble smacked the sidewalk. The dog flinched, ran a short distance away, and sat down on the sidewalk again. I threw another stone. "Get away! Get away!" I screamed.

I didn't wait to see what happened. I sped toward the woods as fast as I could. The wind from my running blew tears back along my face in cold streaks. But I couldn't afford to cry much. I had to be able to see. If it was the last thing I ever did, I'd find the unner and make it work.

I ran down the path, my high tops skidding on leaves slick with half-melted frost. At the big flat-topped rock I stood panting while I tried to remember every move I'd made the night before.

A voice drifted through the red and yellow trees. "Gib, Gib! Wait up!" Ash burst into sight. "Didn't you hear me?"

I would have said no, but I couldn't get my vocal cords to work. They felt locked in ice so cold it burned.

Ash stood very still, looking at me. "Roxy? . . ." he said, his voice breaking off in the middle.

I'd rather have eaten dirt than cried in front of Ash. But it happened anyway. I tried to hold it back and couldn't.

Ash stood there scratching a place on his leg that probably didn't itch as much as it appeared to. It's simple if somebody's crying for a reason that's not very good. You can just shrug and get on with whatever you're doing until they stop acting like a baby. But I had a good reason, and Ash knew it.

"Bad news, huh?" he said. He sat down on the big rock, watching me and waiting for me to tell him.

I went and sat next to him, scrubbing at my eyes while my voice unfroze. "She's got brain damage. The doctors say she'll never wake up."

He sat silent for a long moment, looking as if he'd been slugged in the stomach. I knew exactly how he felt. After a little while, he picked up a twig and broke it in half. "Jeez," he said.

I nodded, feeling completely miserable. "I have to find the unner. It's my only chance."

Ash looked puzzled. "What's the unner?"

"Well, it's like this. . . ." I said, and told him the whole story of the weird old man, his mysterious gift, and what had happened the previous afternoon. "He said it would give me the Power of Un, the power to undo my mistakes, just like on a computer."

Ash cocked one eyebrow. "Are you serious? How do you know the old man wasn't just . . . you know . . . some demented weirdo? Or working for Madam Isis, like I said last night?"

"He smelled like lightning, Ash. Lightning! How could an ordinary demented weirdo smell like lightning? And what about the message he gave Madam Isis? He knew about Roxy's accident before it ever happened."

Ash whistled softly. "You mean, if you find this thing, the unner, and it's real. . . ." He blinked as if he couldn't quite believe what he was about to say. "You mean you could undo the whole thing? Go back and do it over without mistakes? You could make it so Roxy's O.K. again?"

I thought about it a minute, afraid to let myself hope too much. "Well, maybe," I said. "He told me there were limits, though he didn't say what they were. He had to leave before he could show me how it worked. And . . ." I swallowed as the facts came back with unpleasant clarity. "I tried and couldn't get it to work just before I dropped it."

Ash jumped to his feet. "What are we waiting for? Show me where you dropped it, and we can both look. We'll find it! And maybe between the two of us, we can make it work."

I retraced my steps along the path. "Look for a root or a rock—something that might have tripped me," I said.

Before long, we spied a patch of disturbed leaves. Not only that. We found a thick root running across the path. It had to be the spot. We both got down on our hands and knees and started searching as fast as we could.

A few minutes later, Ash whooped and shouted, "Hey, is this it?" I looked over, and there, held aloft like a torch in his hand, was a gunmetal gray box about the size of a paperback book. The unner!

Ash sat cross-legged on the ground as he brushed away dirt and twigs and shook the unner gently to see if it rattled, which it did. "Jeeminy," he said. "Are you sure this is it? I mean . . . well . . . it kind of looks like a piece of garbage."

"Yeah, that's it! Here. Let me see it." I reached to take it from his hands.

Ash shook his head. "Look at this thing. It's crooked, it's taped together, and it rattles. I dunno . . ."

He was right. In the bright light of day, it looked even more homemade than it had the night before. He peered over my shoulder as I punched the keys again, still without results. "There's no zero," he said.

"Yeah, I know. The old guy was in a really big hurry when he made this thing." I kept punching keys. Just as before, nothing happened. What was I doing wrong?

Then it hit me. If this were a game or a calculator or just about any other kind of electronic device, it would have an on/off button. Trembling all over, I ran my fingers around the sides, then felt a tiny raised switch on the left. I turned the unner and looked closely. It was a sliding switch—very small, shiny black, and unlabeled. I took a deep breath and slid the switch upward.

The little machine began to hum. I couldn't hear it, exactly, but I felt it in the palm of my hand, like the beating of a dragonfly's wings. The display screen glowed dimly in the shade of the trees. Three zeroes appeared on it. And each of the colored buttons in the center lit up, then went dark again, in turn. I jumped as the unner made a brief sound like a miniature silver bell, then returned to humming quietly, as if waiting for instructions.

"Whoa!" said Ash.

A wave of excitement rippled up my spine. It was hard to think straight. Ash whipped his baseball cap off and jammed it into the back pocket of his jeans, which is what he always does when he wants to concentrate. He huddled closer to me so he could see the screen and the control buttons.

"O.K., let's stay calm," he said, his voice shaky. I think he was saying it as much for himself as for me. "We have to do this scientifically."

This seemed reasonable enough. "O.K., but . . . what's our hypothesis?"

"Hypothesis?" Ash stared blankly at the controls. "I don't know."

I stared for a while, too, trying to slow my mind down enough so I could catch some sensible thought before it slipped away. It was an uphill battle. "I wonder what these crazy words mean," I said after a few seconds. "HMODE, MMODE, and SMODE." I looked some more and again noticed the three bold letters beside the screen, one under the other: **H**, **M**, and **S**. "H MODE, M MODE, S MODE?" I punched the small, round, yellow button that said HMODE. It lit up.

"What are you doing?" cried Ash. He sounded horrified.

But I was too engrossed to pay much attention. "I'll bet it's in H mode now, whatever that means." Ash gave me a rabbit punch in the arm. "Ow!" I said. "What'd you do that for?"

"Listen to me! Don't touch anything else yet. For all you know, you could undo your whole life."

I licked my lips. He had a point. On the other hand, I was pretty sure nothing major would happen until I punched the **ORDER** button, which I didn't intend to do. Not yet, anyway. "I think it's O.K.," I said.

Ash leaped to his feet. He's careful with his language. When he says a rude word, you know he's really upset. He said one now and followed it with, "Don't be a moron, Gib! This is way too dangerous."

But everything he said seemed to float past from very far away. "You're acting like Rainy Frogner. Sometimes you have to take risks. I know what I'm doing." I punched the 8 because it was in the middle and it was just as good as any other number. An eight appeared on the display screen, opposite the **H**. I punched the 4. Now the display said 84. I pressed the blue MMODE light; it went on, and the yellow HMODE light went off. I punched 6. A six appeared on the display under the 84 and just to the left of the bold **M**. So I was right. H MODE, M MODE, and S MODE. Whoever made the labels just left out the spaces. But what did the numbers mean? What was I programming the unner to do?

It was Ash who saw it first. "*H, M, S.* Eighty-four hours, six minutes, no seconds. Stop now. Please!" He sounded desperate.

I looked up at him. "How can I? There's no 'clear' key."

A little vein popped up on the side of Ash's head. Before I realized what he was doing, he reached down and switched the unner off. "That's how."

A bird in the tree overhead sang a little song. I probably wouldn't have noticed, except it sounded obnoxiously cheerful and reminded me of the first few notes of "Where, Oh Where Has My Little Dog Gone," which seemed just too ironic.

I turned the unner back on, then stabbed the

SMODE button and the first few numbers my fingers landed on—121, as it happened. Then, before Ash could stop me, I hit the big red **ORDER** button.

WORD PROBLEMS **7**

I closed my eyes, waiting for something major to happen. Maybe unning would feel like skydiving or standing beside the tracks when a fast train passes. Maybe my hair would stand on end and my skin would ripple, or maybe I'd go unconscious and wake up with amnesia.

But no. I didn't feel anything except stupid. After a few seconds, I opened one eye. Nothing was different. I was sitting in exactly the same place in the woods with the unner in my hands. Ash was crouched beside me.

I groaned.

"O.K., let's stay calm," said Ash.

"Oh right, that's what you always say," I retorted. "What a ripoff! This thing's just a hunk of junk."

But Ash was still staring at the unner as if it was

the most fascinating object on the planet. "We have to do this scientifically," he murmured.

I snapped at him. "You already said that!"

"Said what?"

"That we have to do this scientifically."

He rolled his eyes. "I did not."

I stared at him. "You did, too! You said we have to do this scientifically, but when I asked about a hypothesis, you didn't have one."

I doubt Ash could have looked more skeptical if I'd told him the woods were full of talking purple dinosaurs. Under my sweatshirt, the hair on my arms rose slowly as it came to me that when I'd punched the big red button, Ash had been standing up, not crouching.

I looked at the unner. It had stopped humming. The word *RECHARGING* flashed on the display screen, then went out. I'd punched in 121 in S mode. If the unner worked, and if I guessed correctly about the *way* it worked, I'd just undone the most recent hundred and twenty-one seconds of my life. What exactly had happened during those two minutes and one second the last time? I strained to remember every detail. The same two minutes seemed to be happening all over again, except for a few minor differences, most of which originated with me.

I looked at Ash, then down at the unner again. As the truth sank in, a prickly feeling started at my toes and traveled upward till it got to my head and made me dizzy. "It worked!" I said.

"If this is supposed to be funny, it's not," said Ash. "How could it work? You haven't done anything except turn it on."

I grabbed his arm. "Listen to me. I punched in a bunch of numbers and hit the red button. It worked. You don't remember, because . . ." I swallowed. I felt like I had sand in my throat. "Because it hasn't happened yet."

Ash stared at me for a very long moment. He breathed out shakily, maybe because he understood what I was trying to tell him or maybe because he thought I'd gone completely bonkers. I couldn't tell which. "That doesn't make sense. If I can't remember, then how can you? Come on, Gib. Stop joking around."

I felt like screaming. "This isn't a joke! It must have something to do with the way the unner works. I mean, there must be some theory to explain it. It's like the unner moved me backward in time—but only me, the person who was holding it. For everybody else, that little chunk of time hasn't happened yet."

Ash squinted at me, his mouth half open. "Gaaaahhh!" I said. "I'll prove it to you!"

I slid the power switch and hit the square green SMODE button again.

Ash leaped to his feet. "Don't be a moron, Gib! This is way too dangerous," he cried.

I laughed, probably a little hysterically. After all, it was like watching an instant replay of life. I remembered what I'd said before, and I liked it, so I said it again: "You're acting like Rainy Frogner. Sometimes you have to take risks. I know what I'm doing."

This time I keyed in 35. Just before I punched the **ORDER** button, the same bird in the same tree whistled the same four obnoxiously cheerful notes. They still reminded me of "Where, Oh Where Has My Little Dog Gone."

I kept my eyes open this time, which turned out to be a mistake, because I saw the world jerk like a movie about to be eaten by its projector. For a second or two, I thought I was going to barf.

Ash flipped into a crouch beside me with impossible speed, though he didn't seem to notice.

"See?" I shouted. "Now do you believe me?"

But instead of shouting "Yes!" as I hoped he would, he stared at me for a very long moment, exactly the way he had half a minute before. The scene I'd already experienced twice now began to replay itself like a videotape. He breathed out shakily, and I found myself thinking all over again that maybe it was because he finally understood what I was trying to tell him, or maybe it was because he thought I'd gone bonkers.

"You're not making any sense," he said. "Are you O.K.? I mean, seriously, you don't look so good."

"Of course I'm O.K.!" I shouted, which was a lie. I'd never felt so far from O.K. in my whole life. My sister was practically dead, my best friend thought I was nuttier than a Snickers bar, and the unner just seemed to be making things worse. How could I ever get Ash to understand what was happening? Was I going to have to do this entire thing on my own?

"Maybe we should go home," he said. He looked scared. Of me.

I shut my eyes and sucked in a big breath of crisp air. *Stay calm,* I told myself. *There has to be a way.* Then I remembered the bird and its stupid repeating song. It was like the moment when you suddenly understand fractions.

"Are we friends?" I asked. I had to concentrate hard to keep my voice low and steady.

"Yeah. You know we are."

"Then you have to trust me. This is the truth. I swear it on . . . on Roxy. In a few seconds, a bird right here in this tree is going to whistle four notes that sound like the beginning of 'Where, Oh Where Has My Little Dog Gone.' Do you know how I know?"

Ash shook his head.

"I know because the unner works. I've already lived these few seconds. I'm living them over again, right now, because I've already used the unner, and it works, cross my heart and hope to die. You've got to believe me." I grabbed his sleeve, cocked an ear toward the tree, and held my breath, hoping to high heaven that I hadn't accidentally done some little thing during the past thirty seconds that would keep the bird from singing this time.

Too tweet dee tweet, sang the bird.

After a beat or two of stunned silence, Ash wrinkled his nose and said, "How'd you do that?"

"I didn't do it. I mean, I didn't make it happen. I just knew it was going to happen, because I've already lived it. Three times now, as a matter of fact."

He pressed his lips into a line, still not really convinced. I could see he was trying to decide whether I was telling the truth or just messing with him.

"O.K.," he said slowly. "Prove it. Tell me what's going to happen next."

I sighed and closed my eyes, then opened them again. This was beginning to feel like pushing a car uphill. "I can't," I said. Which, unfortunately, was true. The thirty-five seconds I'd unned were over. I was living life just like everybody else again, uncertain what might happen in the next instant.

A tide of angry red crept up Ash's neck into his cheeks. "Oh, right," he snapped. "You can't? Pretty convenient, isn't it? You know, this stinks, Gib. You tell me to trust you, then you jerk me around and lie to me. I don't even know why. Is this your idea of fun? Because if it is, you sure picked a stupid time for it."

My heart thumped against my ribs. Who could blame Ash for reacting like this? My story would have seemed lame to anyone for whom time had been moving along in its usual orderly path. There was only one way to convince him.

I held the unner out. "Here," I said. "Take it. Try it yourself."

He glared at me. Heat flickered in his eyes like candle flames. I could see I'd hurt him, and it made me feel bad inside, even though I hadn't meant to do it. After a long moment, he took the unner from my hand without a word.

Only Ash knows what I did next in some chain of events that he later unned. From my point of view, it was all very simple, though surprising. Suddenly, Ash wasn't mad anymore. He looked at me, grinning as if he'd just gotten the birthday present of his dreams. His hands shook as he clutched the unner.

"It works! I can't believe it! It works!"

I whuffed out a gigantic sigh of relief. "What happened? Tell me!"

Ash looked confused for a second or two, then smiled again and exclaimed, "Oh yeah! You don't remember, because it hasn't happened! Now I totally get it." Then he told me how I'd given him the unner and shown him how to use it; how the two of us had decided how much time to punch in—nine seconds; how he'd hit the big red button, still convinced I was trying to make a fool out of him. Then the world seemed to stop. And when it started again, I was back in the middle of handing him the unner and saying, *Here, take it. Try it yourself.* That's when he knew at last that I was telling the truth.

One thing seemed clear. The only person who could remember what was undone was the person who punched the **ORDER** button. For everyone else, it was as if the unned time had simply never happened at all.

Ash handed the unner back to me. "What now?" he said. "Are you going to do it? I mean, un everything that's happened since . . . you know?"

"Since just before the accident? Yeah. I don't think there's any other way to fix it."

Ash pushed air out softly between his lips. It was almost a whistle but not quite. "Scary," he said.

I nodded. "But then, so's living with Roxy's accident for the rest of my life."

Ash nodded in return. "Stinks," he said. "A bad choice or a worse choice."

I stared at the unner in all its shabby glory. I thought about the wild-haired, limping old man. I thought about the smell of lightning, about how very weird time is and how little we really know about it.

I'd never again be able to look at time as a straight line with an arrow at one end. What I saw instead was a maze more tangled than the roots of an ancient tree—a zillion possible wiggly paths taking off from every single thing I'd ever done in the past or might ever do in the future. I knew if I kept thinking about it I'd probably never be brave enough to use the unner again, and I might go crazy besides.

I wondered why the old guy had gone to the trouble of finding me, Gib Finney, and giving me—of all the millions of people who messed up in any day, in any hour even—a chance to correct my mistake. Maybe in some mysterious way, Roxy's accident was even more important than it felt. Which was just one more reason to follow my heart and use the unner, no matter how scary it seemed.

So I said, "I guess it's better than no choice at all." And I got down to business. I found a twig, and I smoothed a spot on the ground where I could write with it. Then I began trying to figure out exactly how long ago the accident had happened.

I'd forgotten to put on my watch when I got up, but Ash was wearing his. It was 9:15 A.M. Neither he nor I knew for sure what time it was when Roxy and the truck's bumper had had their fateful meeting. But we knew we'd started for the carnival around 7:30.

Ash ran his fingers through his hair absently and squatted down beside me so he could see my dirt scribbles. "I remember it was about 9:15 when the ambulance left the carnival," he said.

"So the accident happened between 7:30 and 9:15 last night," I replied, chewing at the inside of my cheek. "If we said 8:30, would that be safe?"

Ash squinted at nothing. "Eight might be safer."

"So how long has it been since 8:00 last night?" I felt a little panicky. I hate word problems, and this was the most awesome word problem of all time.

"I dunno. Count backward?" said Ash, looking like he wasn't too sure himself. "Let's see, 8:15 A.M., 7:15 A.M. . . ."

"Wait," I said. "Twelve hours ago would be 9:15 last night. So 8:15 would have been thirteen hours, and 8:00 would have been thirteen hours and fifteen minutes."

Suddenly we heard someone calling from the direction of the street. "*Gi-i-i-b!* Gib, where are you?" My mom!

"Hurry up!" said Ash.

I turned on the unner and pressed the HMODE button, but it didn't light up. "What the! . . ." I cried. Nothing happened when I pressed any of the number keys.

"Hurry!" Ash said again. "Try MMODE!"

"All right, already!" Like I really needed him to remind me I didn't have much time. It wasn't helping me think.

The MMODE light came on when I pressed it. But minutes . . . how many *minutes* had passed since the accident? Sixty minutes in an hour. I scratched rapidly in the dirt. Sixty times thirteen plus fifteen . . .

"*Gi-i-i-b!*" came Mom's voice again, closer this time.

A trickle of sweat ran into my eyes. I blinked hard. What was six times three? I couldn't remember. Sixty times thirteen, plus fifteen . . . My stick raised little poofs of dust as I worked. One thousand four hundred twenty-one? Could that be right? I wished I'd had time to check my work, then thought, *Well, it's not such a huge problem. If I make a mistake, I can just use the unner to do it over again.* So I keyed in 1421, the largest number we'd tried yet.

"Wish me luck," I said to Ash.

"That looks weird," he said. "Is the math right?"

But by the time he finished asking, I'd already hit **ORDER**. Just before the world slid away, I glimpsed the mangy mutt watching us from among the trees, its mouth in a crazy grin, its tail slapping the ground.

WADING
THROUGH TIME

All right. I admit it. Math isn't my best subject. Everybody, including my teachers, keeps telling me I'd be great if I'd just be more careful. I understand all the ideas—I even think some of them are fun. It's like math is the most complicated puzzle ever invented—full of patterns and surprises and strange little things to discover. All the same, my math grades aren't so hot. I'm always getting the wrong answers because I forget to carry a one, or I get distracted and say eight times seven is forty-two instead of fifty-six. I'm even worse when I'm under pressure. And I was definitely under pressure.

I kept my eyes closed after I punched the red button this time, waiting for the smell of popcorn and the noise of the rides before I opened them again. Imagine my shock when I heard coughs and rustling papers instead, as a man's voice intoned, "You may dunk the skins in water, pour ammonia onto them from this bottle, expose them to heat and moving air from the blow-dryer, squeeze lemon juice onto them, or devise an experiment of your own. All right now, let's get started."

I opened my eyes and found myself seated in the school science lab, staring at Mr. Maynard. I glanced to my right, and there was Lorraine Frogner at my elbow, scribbling stuff in a notebook as fast as she could. The sun was shining through the windows as bright as could be, and the clock on the wall said 9:34. I had on the T-shirt I'd worn Friday—olive green with a picture of a werewolf—and my watch, which I knew I'd left at home, was on my wrist. My hands were completely empty. The unner was nowhere to be seen.

I patted the pockets of my jeans. Nothing. I scooted my stool back and peered under the lab table. Nothing there except my red backpack and Rainy's turquoise one. I grabbed mine, tugged open the zipper, and began to rummage through it. I was breathing hard and starting to sweat. Where could the unner be? Something had gone terribly wrong.

"I think we should do the lemon juice," said Rainy. "I hate the way ammonia smells." She laid down her pen and gave me a look. "Uh . . . is everything all right?"

Before I could consider the consequences, I found

myself blurting in an angry voice, "Do I look like everything's all right?"

Rainy leaned back and curled her lip. "Sheesh, I'm sorry I asked."

I closed my eyes and tried to make my heart slow down to something resembling normal speed. *Panicking never helped anybody,* I told myself. *Think. What's going on here?*

If I was back in science class, then I'd unned a lot more time than I'd planned. But how much more?

"What's one thousand four hundred twenty-one divided by sixty?" I asked. My tongue made sticky noises because my mouth was so dry.

"Oh right, just off the top of my head?" said Rainy.

I opened my eyes, looked hard at her, and said, "I'm serious."

She frowned, picked up her pen again, and scratched a few figures in the margin of her notebook. "Twenty-three, with a remainder of forty-one."

So that was it. Somehow I'd messed up the math and ended up unning twenty-three hours and forty-one minutes instead of the twelve or thirteen hours I'd expected. I was back in the middle of Friday morning, about to relive the worst day of my life in its entirety. Which explained why I didn't have the unner. The moment in which I currently found myself had happened before Rainy would phone to say she was sick, before I would run into the woods, and before I would meet the old man. I didn't have the unner because the old man wouldn't be giving it to me until later that afternoon.

I scratched absently at the tip of my nose, where I expected to feel the fresh scab from the scrape I'd gotten when I tripped and lost the unner in the woods. But my nose was completely smooth. The thought of knowing, among other things, that I was going to fall down and hurt myself later that day made me woozy.

"Cripes," I muttered, wishing I could lie down someplace. "Cripes!"

"What is *wrong* with you?" asked Rainy.

"Uh . . ." I said. "Uh . . ." A new thought had left me completely paralyzed: what if I accidentally said or did something different this time—something that changed the chain of events enough so the old man didn't show up that afternoon? For all I knew, I'd already messed things up completely just by asking Rainy to do long division for me. I read a story once in which a time traveler accidentally changed the whole future just by killing a butterfly. But I didn't want to change the whole future. I just wanted to save Roxy. And, if possible, I also wanted to get the unner again.

"Nothing's wrong," I said, breathing carefully.

"Huh," said Rainy, unconvinced. "Whatever. So, shall we put some lemon juice on our potato skins?"

"Lemon juice!" I yelped. "No! No! We can't!"

Rainy squinched her face up and stared at me as if I'd developed a rash of green spots.

Hastily I added, "I mean, we can, but let's not." I strained to remember the exact words I'd used yesterday . . . or what felt like yesterday. "Everybody's going to do lemon juice. Let's do something original like put salt on ours."

"Salt?" Rainy frowned. "I dunno. Where would we get salt?"

I pointed. "There's a box on the shelf. I'll go get it." I stood up and walked across the room. Somehow I knew I was doing it exactly the way I'd done it the time before. I could feel a faint force, like a wheel wanting to stay in a groove or the pull of a magnet, that made doing the same things over again just a little easier than changing them. Maybe if I stopped thinking so hard and did what felt easiest, I'd be O.K.

Sometimes you get a feeling, like everything that's happening has happened before. Dad told me one time that there's a French term for it, *déjà vu,* which means "seen before." Boy, did I ever have *déjà vu* now. For the next little while, I let events take place by themselves. I felt almost as if I were hovering somewhere behind my own right shoulder, observing as things I knew would happen actually happened. First I watched myself convince Rainy the salt would be better than the lemon juice. Then I watched myself convince her we ought to spread the skins out instead of piling them up. Then I listened to myself with growing discomfort as I tried to talk her into salting them heavily instead of lightly.

I knew what was coming. We were about to have a fight, and Rainy would end up pouring the whole box of salt in my lap. Then I thought if I changed one thing just a little bit, I might be able to avoid the anger and frustration of being called selfish in front of everybody—and having to clean up the salty mess from under the table. Would that be so bad?

Part of me said yes, it would be bad. Possibly worse than bad. Immoral. What if there was some kind of Master Plan, and I messed it all up? Did I have the right to do something that might change the future of everybody else in the world? I'd be doing it entirely to make my own life easier, and I wasn't asking anybody else what they wanted. It didn't feel right.

But a different part of me—the most persuasive part, as it turned out—thought it was a great idea not to relive this particularly embarrassing scene. So what if Rainy felt a little kinder toward me? I couldn't see how that would change anything major in the long run. Not in a bad way, at least. After all, wasn't this exactly the kind of thing the unner was meant for? If I wasn't supposed to change anything, why had the old man given me the unner in the first place?

So when the time came for me to say, "Come on.

If it gets messy, I'll clean it up," I said something else instead. "O.K., no big deal. Put the salt on whatever way you want."

Rainy smiled and said, "O.K."

After that, everything was spookily different for a while, and I began to wonder if I'd made a gigantic mistake. True, Rainy and I didn't fight. But that also meant we did things we hadn't done before. Instead of crawling around under the table with the whisk broom and the dustpan, we actually finished our experiment and wrote up the results in our notebooks. And those results were boring, just as I'd originally feared—there wasn't enough salt to draw the water out, so nothing much happened.

Toward the end of the period, things started to get familiar again. The bell rang. We picked up our back-packs and headed down the hall to other classes. I met up with Ash, who had no idea the unner existed. We talked about our carnival plans and tried to make each other bump into walls as we walked to gym.

Things went exactly as they had before. I grinned and felt muscles in my arms and shoulders loosen that I hadn't even realized were tight. I'd used the Power of Un to rescue myself from one of the worst parts of the day, and still I was in a chain of known events, and everything was going along just fine. Maybe time was like a pool of water: when you disturb it, ripples go out from the place you touched—strong in the center, but getting fainter and fainter, till finally you can't see them anymore.

I hoped I was right. But I couldn't be sure. So I made a pact with myself not to change things carelessly. Making changes felt bad, like cheating. I also didn't want to get lost and find myself in a future even worse than the one I knew was coming. It seemed strange to think such a thing, because after all, what could be worse than Roxy getting hit by a truck? But I could imagine worse possibilities: both of us getting hit by a truck, or Mom and Dad getting hit by a truck, or an earthquake, or our house burning down with all of us in it.

The trouble is, as the hours passed and things continued to happen just as I remembered, I got kind of overconfident. All those awful scenarios faded into the background until they seemed so overblown and unlikely that I stopped worrying about them. Probably I'd already done a bunch of stuff differently without even realizing it, and so far there were no problems at all. How much could it hurt if I changed a few tiny things on purpose?

When I went through the lunch line, I asked for macaroni and cheese, because I remembered that the potatoes and gravy had tasted putrid. It didn't make one speck of difference that I could see, except that I liked my lunch better. Feeling pleased with myself, I gave in to temptation and made another small change later, on the playground. I stepped out of the way instead of getting whapped in the stomach by a stray dodge ball.

Ash said, "Whoa! That was great! How'd you see it coming?"

I grinned and said, "I dunno. Instinct, I guess."

Then things started to get weird. Instead of bouncing off my middle and scudding back toward the kid who threw it, the dodge ball sped toward an open gate.

"Hey, catch that ball!" the kid yelled.

"Sure thing," Ash called, and he ran after it. For one awful moment I was sure he would chase that ball into the street and run in front of a truck. But it didn't happen that way. He caught the ball before it got through the gate and threw it back to the players. Still, the scare left me struggling to keep that macaroni and cheese in my stomach where it belonged.

I tried to get things back on track and insisted we go to the computer lab, even though Ash wanted to stop for a drink of water on the way. The awful possibilities sprang into clear focus again. Who could say what might happen if he stopped for that drink? After a few minutes, events began to happen the way I expected, and I could breathe normally again. But I renewed my vow not to change anything else.

Minute followed minute until the end of the day finally arrived and it was time for Ms. Shripnole's math class once more. Ash and I passed notes to each other instead of doing our decimals work sheets, and when I opened my binder for more paper, the soda straw fell out. I gritted my teeth and picked it up, knowing exactly how uncomfortable the next few moments would be. I even started to make the fateful spitball. Then I thought, *This is going to be horrible. Maybe it's worth it to risk another change. Maybe if I don't shoot this spitball, Rainy won't get into trouble. Then she won't have any reason to get mad at me. She'll come and baby-sit instead of pretending to be sick, and Roxy will never get near the carnival or the bumper of that horrendous truck. Maybe this is the one small mistake that, if avoided, will make the big things right again. Maybe I'm supposed to change this! But am I brave enough to try it? If the spitball incident never happens, everything might go differently. Suppose the new time path I make creates some of those awful situations I've imagined? There I might be, and Roxy, too, at fate's mercy again, maybe without the unner, or any hope of ever getting it.*

I thought it all through at light speed while I held the soda straw in one hand and the spitball in the other. I wanted to do the best thing this time. I should never have shot that dumb spitball. It felt right to avoid it now.

A second passed, then two. I laid the straw down and dropped the spitball on the floor.

Halfway through a smile of relief, I glanced over at

Rainy. The smile froze on my face like a lopsided Popsicle. Rainy had just shot her own spitball. Only she didn't aim it at me this time. I honestly think she was trying for the blackboard or one of the lights. Who knows what made her do it? She wasn't angry at me now. Maybe she was just in the mood for a little excitement. Even a girl like Rainy might get bored in math class on a too-warm Friday afternoon. But she hadn't had much practice with spitballs, or with sneakiness. The wet wad hit Ms. Shripnole in the center of the forehead, right where mine had hit her before. Rainy sat with her mouth half open and the straw in her hand, a sitting duck.

Ol' Shrapnel's face went through its series of expressions. It was like watching the Wheel of Fortune, knowing it would land on FURY. "Lorraine Frogner!" she roared.

I don't remember thinking much about what I did next. I'd decided I was going to change this scene, and I could see that nothing would end up being very different unless I took further action. This, more than anything else, convinced me of the importance of the moment. Something big was fighting me, trying to keep things the way they were.

I felt as if I were pushing my way through Jell-O instead of air as I pulled out my hidden soda straw and stood up. I spoke slowly and clearly, not because I wanted to, but because it took an effort to move my tongue. "Ms. Shripnole, it's not Lorraine's fault," I said. "I shot the spitball."

HEARTS AND UNNINGS

Everything stopped. Nobody said a word. Ash, frozen in the act of chewing his pencil, stared at me as if he couldn't decide whether I'd gone crazy or he had. Rainy Frogner held perfectly still, her mouth half open. So did Ms. Shripnole. They looked like impossible twins. Outside, the school custodian, Mr. Beeter, pruned shrubbery. He was whistling "If I Only Had a Brain," and the classroom was so unnaturally quiet, you could hear every note.

Ms. Shripnole blinked and looked at me, then at Rainy, then at me again. Pink crept up her neck toward her face, as if she were slowly filling with strawberry Kool-Aid. She reached up, pinched the spitball from her forehead, and dropped it on my desk.

"Please pick that up, Gibson," she said in a voice so soft it made my veins feel icy.

I gulped and picked it up. It was cold, wet, and completely disgusting. And it was Rainy Frogner's spit, which made it even worse.

Ms. Shripnole grasped me firmly by the arm and pulled me to my feet—not angrily, exactly, just deliberately. She was surprisingly strong. I wished I could disappear under my desk.

Her gaze shifted to Rainy, and she said, "Lorraine, it seems I was mistaken. I apologize." Then she looked at me again. No, that's not quite right. She *glared* at me. "I believe Gibson would like to apologize, too." Her hand tightened around my arm.

"Uh . . ." I said.

Rainy's eyebrows pulled together. The soda straw between her fingers trembled slightly. So did her lower lip. "But, but . . ." she stammered.

I could see she was going to burst into tears and say she'd done it, which would ruin my whole plan. "I apologize!" I practically shouted. "I shouldn't have shot the spitball, and I'm sorry you got blamed."

She opened her mouth, but nothing came out. Maybe she was stunned. I mean, she must have thought I was suffering from mental illness.

I thought, *I really, really, really hope I'm doing this right, and I really, really, really hope it's going to be worth it.*

Ms. Shripnole's grip relaxed slightly. "Because

you've been truthful, Gibson, I won't send you to the principal's office this time. But if you ever shoot another spitball in this classroom, don't expect further forbearance. Please be seated, and speak to me after class."

She let go of my arm, and I sat down gladly, because my knees were shaking. "Yes, ma'am," I said. I picked up my pencil and bent over my decimals work sheet. My face felt hot as a campfire. I knew every kid in the classroom must be staring at me. Ash, who sat in the desk behind mine, kicked my foot.

When I glanced over my shoulder at him, he gave me a look that said, *Are you out of your mind?*

"Tell you later," I whispered. As I sat there trying to figure out the answer to 40.587364 divided by 1.7337618112, I realized that if I told him, I'd seem even crazier than I already did. This time I couldn't convince him by just giving him the unner and telling him to use it himself.

I shivered, even though rivulets of sweat were meandering down my back. I was scared, and in a weird way, I felt more alone than I ever had before in my life.

The bell rang, and everybody else packed up their books. The room filled with talk and laughter and a few shouts of joy as kids crowded out through the door. Ash frowned at me and said, "What are you doing? Do you *want* to be in trouble or something?"

"No!" I replied. "Trust me. I have my reasons. I'll explain later. See you tonight."

"Whatever you say." He shrugged and shook his head as he left the room, probably thinking my brain was experiencing total system failure.

I sighed, trying to get myself psychologically prepared to talk to Ol' Shrapnel and find out what kind of punishment she had in store for me. I looked down at my desk. There sat a piece of pink paper, folded into a tiny square. I glanced around the room, wondering where it had come from. All the kids were gone. I unfolded it, and inside was a note, written in purple pen:

> Thank you SO-O-O-O much. You are the nicest boy I know.
>
> Yours truly,
>
> Lorraine

Each letter was perfectly formed in Rainy's careful, round handwriting, for which she'd won a citywide award the year before. A plump heart dotted the *i* over *nicest*. I groaned.

Ol' Shrapnel's punishment was suitably hideous. I had to write one hundred times: *If I had not told the truth about the spitball, I would have to write this two hundred times instead of one hundred.* I wasn't allowed to put 100 or 200. I had to spell them out. And I had to have it finished by Monday morning.

I walked home, and as I turned up the path to our front door, my stomach started feeling like a cave full of bats. The last time I'd been through that door, Dad was at Roxy's bedside in the hospital, and Mom was crying herself to pieces as she learned Roxy would never wake up again—a complete nightmare. My brain knew that in the current version of reality, none of that had happened yet. But the rest of me wasn't so sure.

I turned the knob and stuck my head into the entryway, my heart banging. "Hi," I called, trying to sound nonchalant. "I'm home."

"Hi!" Dad called from the kitchen, his voice happy and hearty. The smell of simmering beef stew hung in the air like a promise. Maybe everything really was all right again.

I carefully set my backpack on the hall table, licked my lips, and said, "Where's Roxy?"

I didn't realize I was holding my breath until she came speeding around the corner in her stocking feet. She slid over the polished floor like a batter going for home plate and ran right into me. "Gib! You're home! You're home!" she cried.

"Rox! Am I ever glad to see you!" I blurted before I realized how unlike myself it would be to say such a thing. I wasn't even mad that she'd almost knocked me over.

She looked up at me, eyebrows high. "Really?" she said.

I laughed. I couldn't stop myself, not that I wanted to. In fact, I felt like I might burp rainbows any second.

I was happy and I knew it, and weirdest of all, I didn't care who else knew it, either. "Hey, would you like to play doggy?"

Roxy's wide, bright eyes narrowed to suspicious slits. "You're kidding, right?"

"No, I'm serious. Let's play doggy! I'll go get the leash."

"Aw-ri-i-i-ght!" she said. "Whuff!" She let her tongue loll out and began to pant.

Dad stuck his head around the kitchen doorway and chuckled. "Boy, I guess somebody had a good day today."

I smiled, struck by the general greatness of the way my dad chuckles. Saturday morning I'd thought he might never smile again, let alone chuckle. "Yeah, a really good day," I said.

As I walked to Roxy's bedroom to get the leash, I thought how weird it was for me to feel this had been a good day—after all, tucked into my backpack, Ol' Shrapnel's spitball-punishing assignment lay in wait. I guess some days feel good mainly because other days are so bad.

So I played doggy with Roxy, and though I wouldn't say it was actually fun, it didn't feel as much like a chore as usual. I kept looking at Roxy and thinking how great it was that she could run around laughing, her whole body working perfectly.

Afterward, I went out and shot hoops again, trying

to stick to the original chain of events as closely as I could. I wasn't sure if I could still get the unner—things were already so different from before. But I figured it couldn't hurt.

When it was about time for me to walk to the woods, I went back into the house, feeling jittery again. Would Dad be on the phone with Rainy? Would she be telling him she'd come down with the flu?

Dad's voice drifted out of the kitchen. He wasn't on the phone with Rainy. Instead he was singing a somewhat cracked version of a square-dance tune.

Rainy *was* going to baby-sit. Ash and I could go to the carnival without Roxy, and she would be safe, safe, safe! I nearly whooped with joy. My plan was working.

I told Dad I was going over to the woods for a while. Just as before, he reminded me to be back in time for dinner.

"No problem," I said. "See you soon."

I found the empty Coke can in front of our house, and this time, instead of kicking it, I picked it up and tossed it in the air, running to catch it, imagining what it would be like to be a star receiver in the NFL. I did that all the way to the woods and was feeling so good I nearly forgot I'd ever been worried about using the unner. It was beginning to look like smooth sailing from here on out, whether the old man reappeared or not. If he didn't, Roxy would still be O.K. If he did, I'd get the unner back and be invincible. I could make everything happen the way I wanted for the rest of my life. In fact, I might even find a way to live forever!

I started down the leaf-crunchy path, looking left and right. I was just about to give up when the old man stepped out of the shadows between two tree trunks.

He looked just as strange as he had before. His shiny, silvery hair stood out around his head as if he'd rubbed it with a party balloon. Pale vapor and the weird electrical smell rose from his rumpled coat.

"Hi!" I said, as if I'd known him forever, which, silly though it may seem, was exactly the way I felt. "How are you doing?"

He leaned back and laughed. "You're not so scared this time, eh?"

"Wha . . . you remember last time?" I said, my voice a startled squeak. It hadn't occurred to me that he might remember events that had happened before I unned them. Nobody else did. Suddenly I *was* a little afraid of him again. My head filled with all the forgotten questions that remained stubbornly unanswered.

He nodded. "Yes, I remember. Let's find that flat rock again, shall we? I need to sit down. Jumping around like this is hard on my knee. Old injury." He smiled like someone who had a huge secret, beckoned, and started down the path in his slow, uneven way.

"Jumping around?" I asked. I hadn't noticed him jumping around at all.

"Well, in a manner of speaking. I don't mean 'jumping around' in the literal sense. I mean, 'jumping around' in the . . ." He waved a hand through the air. "Haven't thought of a word for it yet." He glanced at the back of his hand, as he had before, and I got a better look at the shiny, flat panel set into his skin. A small, lighted display of numbers flashed across it in neon green.

"What's that?" I asked.

His eyes twinkled. "Pretty cool, huh? It's kind of like a watch, but not really. Some things never change. I still don't have much time."

There they were again—words nobody his age should be using. *Cool. Kind of.*

I tugged at his arm, and we stopped in the middle of the path. "Who are you? How come you remember things I unned, when nobody else does? How come you gave the unner to me and not some other person?"

He looked at me for a second or two, chewing his lower lip in a thoughtful way. Then he turned and started walking again. "I know you're full of questions. Some of them I can answer. Some I can't. Some you haven't even thought of yet. Not that I wouldn't like to tell you everything. Speaking of the unner . . ." He reached into the folds of his coat and pulled out the little gray box. It looked just the same as it had before. Our progress toward the rock slowed down as he struggled to give it to me. I could see his muscles tightening as he strained to place it in my hands.

He looked at me, half frowning, half grinning, his eyes full of excitement. "I've been thinking about why this is so hard," he said. "Time is like most things. You need energy to change it. The more you change it, the more energy it takes, and this is a big change. Also, the farther you are from what you want to change, the more energy it takes, and I'm farther from the event than you are." The half grin disappeared from his face, and only the frown was left. "Oops. I probably shouldn't have said that."

"Farther from what event? Shouldn't have said what?"

"Nothing. Nothing," he replied. With a final hard shove, he once again succeeded in handing me the unner.

I thanked him, though I'm sure I didn't sound as grateful as I should have. I was just so curious about him and so frustrated by his refusal to tell me anything I could really sink my teeth into. It was hard to be polite.

"Be extra careful with it," he said. "It's even more important this time."

That stopped me dead in my tracks. "What do you mean?"

He shrugged.

Invisible ants scuttled along my backbone as

everything suddenly fell into place. "You know my future! You're *from* the future, aren't you?"

I've replayed this scene in my mind a thousand times since then, trying to remember every tiny detail. Looking back on it now, I know it was one of the most important moments of my life.

We'd come to the rock, and he sat down on it. A small, sympathetic smile crossed his face. "Yes, I know your future and a lot more," he said. "You want me to tell you what's going to happen tonight, tomorrow, five years from now. You want to know how I know. All I can say is that if I told you, the consequences might be more awful than you can imagine. I've already taken terrible risks, telling you as much as I have, doing as much as I have. So don't ask. Just take the unner with you tonight. Don't drop it in the leaves. Most important of all, don't use it unless you have to."

I rubbed my thumb across the unner where the front of the case met the back and the black tape ran around them both in a sticky ridge.

The old man stood up and put one hand on each of my shoulders. In spite of his age, he was tall, and an atmosphere of power and excitement surrounded him. "It looks homemade because I made it in a hurry. And I made it for a reason so awesome you wouldn't believe it if you knew it. You're more important than you know, Gib. And so is Roxy. Everything depends on you."

He touched his forehead in a kind of salute. Among the trees, I caught the same shadowy, almost invisible motion I'd seen the last time he gave me the unner, just as he disappeared.

"You're going?" I said in a voice like a rusty hinge.

"I have to. Do you see my colleagues in the lab?" He pointed toward the wavering figures among the shadows. "They're only visible because the time bubble is deteriorating. Like I said before, we're not very good at this yet." He shuffled backward slowly. "I won't see you again unless something goes terribly wrong. But I want you to know . . ." He was fading even as I watched. ". . . I want you to know I trust you. And I'm proud of you."

It was a long time before I turned and made my way carefully through the twilight, back to Cherrywood Drive and a life that would never be the same.

WHAT IS AND
WHAT ISN'T?

I walked in slow motion, squinting through the twilight at my high tops half hidden in the deep litter of fallen leaves, stepping around rocks and roots whenever I saw them, even if they were small. I kept the unner tucked under my arm in a snug hold, as if it were a football and I were on my way to the end zone in the biggest game ever. All the while, my mind was going a million miles a minute.

The old man knew my future—and Roxy's. He had to be from the future. It fit perfectly. If he was a time traveler, all kinds of things about him began to make sense—the display panel on the back of his hand, his strange clothes, his sudden appearances and disappearances, and the fact that he often arrived looking and smelling as if he'd just had a close encounter with enough electricity to light a major city for a week. Most of all, it offered a clue about why he'd given the unner to me rather than to one of the zillion or so other people on the planet who appeared to be much more powerful and important. Some events are a lot more momentous than they seem. I knew that from the spitball incident. Maybe some people are more momentous than they seem, too.

You're important in the world, and so is Roxy. Everything depends on you. There was something ominous about the way he'd said it. Something BIG. It was hard to hold onto such a scary idea. I wasn't sure I wanted to be so important that someone from the future would go to the trouble of inventing the unner and traveling through time to deliver it to me—not once, but *twice.* And I definitely didn't want everything to depend on me! What did I know? I was just a kid, after all. I thought Roxy was already saved, but if I still needed the unner, maybe I was mistaken about that. Or maybe Roxy's accident was the wrong thing to undo. Maybe some other event was the key. How was I supposed to know? I didn't want to think about it, because it felt like standing on the edge of a cliff. Why hadn't he just told me what to do?

Since I wasn't late for dinner and didn't have a scraped nose, the whole scene with Mom at the front door just dropped out of existence. I hid the unner in my bedroom, then went straight to the kitchen to eat. Mom was in the bathroom when I arrived, probably putting on makeup or messing around with her sequins. Dad sat with us, whistling and pulling on his cowboy boots while we ate. Roxy talked nonstop.

"Oh boy, Rainy's coming over, and it's going to be so much fun, *so much fun,* I can hardly wait, she'll play doggy with me, I know she will because she always does, and Mommy says Rainy's going to take me to the carnival, so nyah nyah to you, Gib, you're not the only one who gets to go. . . ."

"Wha–*What?*" I croaked and dropped my spoon. Stew splattered everywhere. "What did you say?"

"Golly, Gib! Watch what you're doing!" said Dad, clomping to the counter to tear off a paper towel. He'd only succeeded in getting one boot on.

"I . . . sorry . . . I . . . Roxy, did you say you're going to the carnival?"

"Yeah, nyah nyah!" she said, sticking her tongue out between grinning lips.

"Roxy, stop that. It's rude. Behave, you two!" Dad growled as he handed me the towel. "Clean up the mess you made, my friend."

"But, Dad!" I said as I swiped at spilled stew. "She can't go to the carnival. She just can't!"

"What do you mean?" said Dad. "Of course she can. I think it's wonderful that Lorraine offered to take her."

"No. No! You don't understand. It's . . ." A little groan accidentally escaped my throat, along with a couple of sentences I didn't mean to say aloud. "It's way too dangerous, don't you see? Do you want it to happen all over again?"

Dad froze in the midst of pulling on his second boot. "Want *what* to happen all over again?"

"The acci—" I barely stopped myself. My voice trailed off into embarrassed silence. A second passed, then two, while little beads of sweat popped out on my chin. I gulped and tried to start over again. "I mean . . . she might get hurt. Little kids get hurt all the time at carnivals." Which sounded pretty lame, even to me. Actually, I'd *never* heard of a little kid getting hurt at a carnival.

I guess Dad hadn't, either. "Gib, what's this all about?"

I jammed my hands into my pockets to keep him from seeing how shaky they were. "I dunno. It's just too dangerous, that's all."

He looked at me as if I'd announced that saving the rain forests wasn't worth the trouble. "It sounds to me like you don't want your sister to go and you're having difficulty thinking up good reasons for it. Wouldn't you say that's just a little bit selfish?"

"That's not it at all! You don't understand." I wished I were on the far side of the galaxy.

Luckily, Mom walked into the kitchen just then.

She was in the process of putting on a pair of armadillo-shaped earrings by feel, and she seemed a little distracted. "Gib's just worried, honey. That's not selfish. In fact, it's kind of sweet." She planted a kiss on my cheek, then said, "Darn lipstick," and rubbed the spot with licked fingers while I squirmed. "Don't worry, kiddo. Rainy won't let anything happen. Roxy's completely safe with her. If Dad and I weren't certain of it, we wouldn't let her go."

Roxy watched all this with interest, then grinned at me and said, "Nyah nyah," again.

"Behave!" Dad repeated.

The doorbell rang, and there stood Rainy, her arms full of schoolbooks. Even though it was Friday night, she'd be doing homework as soon as Roxy went to bed. I wondered if she ever gave herself a break.

"Hi, Mr. and Mrs. Finney. Hi, Roxy." She smiled at me, looked at the floor, and added, "Hi, Gib."

It didn't exactly take mighty powers of observation to see what she was thinking—with big hearts over both *i*'s. I stopped myself from groaning just in time. It would have been idiotic, especially in front of Mom and Dad. More to the point, there was still plenty of room for things to go wrong if Rainy got mad at me again. Somehow I was going to have to stay on her good side without making her think I liked her.

I mumbled, "Hi, how're you?" while I panicked inside.

Dad helped Mom into her fringed, sequined jacket, and she picked up her red-white-and-blue purse. Major *déjà vu*.

"Bye, kids," she said, blowing us kisses. "Have a wonderful time."

Dad, all smiles again, said, "Roxy, behave for Lorraine. Gib, make sure you're in by ten. And don't worry so much. Everything'll be fine." He slapped me on the shoulder, which meant I was forgiven and all was well. But he didn't know the future.

When I'd closed the front door behind them, I turned to Rainy. "Um . . . so you're thinking of taking Roxy to the carnival."

"Yeah, I thought it might be fun," she said. She smiled in Roxy's direction, and her face got soft and happy. It came to me that she really liked my sister. Roxy can be such a pain, I guess it hadn't occurred to me that Lorraine might baby-sit her because she actually enjoyed spending time with her.

"Could you come out to the living room?" I asked.

Roxy looked up from her stew. "I'm coming, too!"

In days of yore, I would have just told her no and commanded her to stay there and finish her dinner. But after the accident, bossing her around wasn't much fun anymore. So instead I said, "If you finish your stew, I'll try to win a stuffed dog for you at the carnival. Deal?"

Roxy's eyes went wide. "Deal!" she said, and she got busy with her spoon. One more crisis averted.

I looked at Rainy. "Please? I have to talk to you about something . . . in private."

Rainy's cheeks got red, and she stared at the floor again. "Oh, you mean that note?" she mumbled.

My own cheeks got hot as I realized I'd just made a strategic error. I floundered around, trying to think of something I could say that was true but not too insulting: *I only acted like a dimwit in shining armor because I had to? No, I totally do not want to talk about that dumb note?*

Desperation set in.

I heard myself say, "Oh. Well, thank you for the note. Um, it's nice to know you think I'm nice."

Rainy's face lit up like a birthday cake. "It was so great what you did, I mean, getting me out of trouble like that, even though you had to take the blame unfairly."

"Well . . . thanks, but . . ." I scratched around the neck of my T-shirt, which suddenly itched and felt way too hot. "You know, it probably wasn't as great as it seemed." That was pretty much the understatement of the year.

"Oh yes, it was. You're a really good person, Gib."

I smiled. I couldn't help it. It feels pretty terrific when somebody tells you you're a good person and means it as absolutely as she did at that moment.

A second later, though, she ruined the whole thing. Taking me completely by surprise, she darted in as fast as an attacking bat and kissed me on the cheek!

We both stood there for a couple of seconds, stunned. I reached up and started to rub it off, then stopped myself. Rubbing off the kiss might make her mad. I nearly groaned again and had to stop myself from doing that, too. Things had gone from sticky to hideous.

Rainy was no longer looking at me. She stared hard at the floor again, but I could still see that her cheeks were red as Atomic Fire Balls. I was pretty sure mine were, too.

I cleared my throat. It seemed like a good time to change the subject to what I'd been wanting to talk to her about all along: Roxy, the carnival, and the Truck of Terror. The problem was, what exactly could I say? *The Great and Powerful Gib knows all, sees all, Roxy is in great danger tonight?*

I took a deep breath. "Look, I . . . this is going to sound really weird, but . . . well . . . I need your help tonight."

"My help?" said Rainy. To her credit, the look on her face wasn't lovesick. It was somewhere between puzzled and suspicious, which seemed sort of like progress and gave me hope.

"It's . . . it's about the carnival. If you take Roxy over there, please, whatever you do, don't let go of her. Not even for a second."

"What?" Rainy wrinkled her nose. "She's not a two-year-old. How's she supposed to play a game or have fun on the rides if I can't let go of her? What's this all about?"

I scratched my neck so hard she probably wondered if I had fleas. "This is hard to explain. Don't ask me how I know, because you wouldn't believe me even if I could tell you. But Roxy's in terrible danger. There's this stray dog at the carnival. Roxy loves dogs, and she might run after it, right into the street . . ." I stopped because Rainy was staring at me with her eyebrows up and her mouth slightly open.

Finally she said slowly and carefully, as if I might be too sick to hear her, "I'm supposed to hold on to your sister like a prison guard because she might run after a dog? Do you feel all right?"

"Yes, I'm fine!"

She didn't reply. She just stood there looking at me. I could tell she was trying to figure out what in the world was going on in my head, and nothing she'd thought of made any sense. Not that I could blame her.

I sighed and scratched my neck some more. "O.K., then, it doesn't matter why. Just . . . just don't let Roxy run into the street. It's really, *really* important."

This turned out to be the wrong thing to say.

Rainy threw her books on the couch and planted her hands on her hips, her shyness and embarrassment suddenly sizzling into storm clouds. "Do you think I'm an idiot? I'm not going to let her anywhere near the street. You think I would let a six-year-old run into the street?"

The look she gave me was so angry I put my hands up to shield myself from it. So much for pink notes and hearts!

"No! That's not what I meant at all," I said, and this time I did groan, because the look on her face didn't change even a little. I'd managed to get her mad in spite of myself, and trying to fix it was only making it worse. "Forget it," I said. "I know you'll take good care of her. My mistake."

I probably should have added something polite, like *have a nice night,* or *see you at the carnival.* But the whole situation had begun to feel like standing inside a beehive. So I turned without another word and walked to my bedroom. I slid the unner into the pocket of my baseball jacket and ran out the front door. My warning still might make Rainy extra careful, I thought. If it didn't, I'd just have to come up with a different way to solve the problem. I took a huge breath of cool, dark air and headed down the street toward Ash's house.

I knocked on the Jensens' front door and felt weird when Ash's dad answered it. I half expected him to ask me if I was feeling better now, because the last time I'd seen him was the night of Roxy's accident. But of course none of that had ever happened as far as he knew. It was just an ordinary Friday night to him, and

I was just the ordinary neighbor kid from a perfectly ordinary, happy family. I stood in the entryway a few minutes waiting for Ash, peeking toward the living room and a scene so cheery it looked like a calendar painting. Ash's parents were playing Scrabble at a low table in front of the wood stove and laughing a lot.

Before long Ash and I were walking side by side through the autumn night toward Lafferty Park and the carnival. Ash was so excited he could hardly stop talking. "Oh man, I hear the people on the rides! Smell the popcorn? Hey, Gib, what should we do first? How about the Devil's Elevator!"

It's hard to describe how much I wanted to feel just the way Ash did—bursting with joy at the prospect of so much fun right around the corner. But I'd done it once already, and it had ended in blood and tears. It was impossible to forget, and I wouldn't have wanted to forget it anyway. If I forgot about it, how could I stop it from happening again? There was also the fact, like a constant itch in the back of my brain, that the unner sat right there in my pocket. I had this incredible device that Ash had helped me learn to use. But now he knew absolutely nothing about it. I couldn't stand it another second.

"Ash, look, stop a minute," I said. "I have to tell you something."

He stood still and really looked at me for the first time that evening. "What's wrong?"

I sighed and took the unner out of my pocket.

The scene that followed was eerily similar to the one in the forest that had happened . . . when? Well, the scene that might have happened the next morning in some other life. As I showed Ash the unner, I felt that strange pressure that meant I was changing the way things had originally happened. And I wondered again whether I, or anyone else, had a right to do such a thing. There didn't seem to be an answer.

We sat in silence on the curb while dead leaves whirled along the pavement in a breeze that came and went.

"This is very weird," said Ash.

"You're telling me."

"You mean, if you hadn't stood up and taken the blame for Frogner's spitball this afternoon, Roxy would be run over by a truck tonight?"

I nodded. "The thing is, I'm not sure that really fixed it. I think something bad is still going to happen. Otherwise, why would the old guy have brought me the unner again and given me those warnings? I mean, *Take the unner with you tonight, don't drop it in the leaves, and most important of all, don't use it unless you have to.* Why would he do and say all that if he didn't know there was more bad stuff to come?"

Ash shook his head, gazing at something faraway and invisible. "You think he was from the future?"

"It's the only thing that makes any sense."

He looked at me. "You wanna know what I think?"

"What?"

"I think he's you. I think the old man is you visiting yourself from the future."

"What?" I said again, stupidly, because I felt as if somebody had suddenly turned on a light in a dark room, and everything looked completely different from what I expected.

"He's you. Think about it. That's how he knows so much about you and Roxy. That's how he knew you'd be in the woods."

Why hadn't I thought of it before? It explained everything. But . . . "How could he be me?" I said. "I mean, he's so . . . so old. And shriveled. And weird!"

"I think it's pretty cool, myself, if it's true," said Ash. "My best friend is the guy who invents time travel. So what if you turn out weird? Big surprise." He flashed a grin.

I punched him, and he punched me back, and we both laughed. I still couldn't quite believe it, though. I just couldn't imagine myself being like that when I got old.

Ash stood up and dusted off his hands. "Come on, we'd better get over to the carnival fast," he said. "That way, you and me and Rainy can all keep an eye on Roxy. And if anything bad happens, we'll be right there with the unner to fix it again."

"Yeah, but how do we know? I mean, how will I ever be sure I'm fixing the right thing? What if Roxy's accident is *supposed* to happen?"

"Get serious," said Ash. "Roxy's accident is not supposed to happen. Bad things are *never* supposed to happen to kids."

I wanted to believe him. I really did. But I thought about stories I'd read in the newspaper and about Roxy and the truck. Bad things did happen to kids. They happened all the time to people who didn't seem to deserve them. I couldn't even start to figure out what it meant to say they weren't *supposed* to happen. How could anybody ever be sure about that?

"Come on!" said Ash. "We might as well have some fun while we're keeping watch!"

He ran toward Lafferty Park, and I jogged along beside him, hoping with all my might that he was right, that Roxy's accident wasn't supposed to happen.

LOSERS WIN,
WINNERS LOSE

There it was, the whole scene all over again—the frantically moving colored lights, the clowns, the vendors swaggering past with big trays on their shoulders, shouting, "Peanuts, popcorn, cotton can-deee." Only this time, instead of filling me with excitement, it made my stomach ache and my mouth go dry.

I sagged against an upright at the coin-toss booth. "I don't think I can do this. It was so awful last time."

"You *can* do it," said Ash. "This is not last time. It's *this* time. And we're going to make sure it's different, right?" He punched me in the arm, leaned crazily, and grinned into my face until I grinned back. I don't know why, but smiling made me feel better.

"So what should we do first?" he asked.

I licked my lips and tried to think. The noise of

the crowd and the powerful music of the carousel made it hard to concentrate. "Maybe we should look around and see if we can spot Roxy and Rainy."

"Sounds good," said Ash.

So we spent some time ambling among the booths. A lot of little things were different this time already. Some rides weren't in the same places, and there was some stuff I didn't remember at all from before. For example, there was a Haunted House right next to the Freaks of Nature and no House of Illusions at all. And Madam Isis's tent was no longer purple and yellow. It was red and black. My stomach started feeling better—maybe this time the night would be different. Maybe this time the mangy mutt wouldn't be here. We bought corn dogs and ate them while we walked.

After half an hour, we still hadn't run across Roxy or Rainy. Then Ash saw a booth with a radio-controlled airplane hanging from the prize rack, and his eyes got huge. "I've always wanted one of those," he said. "I'm going to win that thing!"

The game was one where you try to knock down milk bottles with a baseball, and Ash is a really good pitcher. He knocked a whole bunch down, and the carny notched up the stakes, saying he was working his way closer to the airplane, just another fifty cents was all it would take. Ash was doing great, better than I'd ever seen before. His cheeks glowed, and his eyes flamed with excitement. He seemed to forget about everything else and just kept reaching into his pocket for more and more money, as if he couldn't help himself. He'd spent almost twelve dollars when the carny finally said, "This is it, chief. Knock this one down and you get the plane."

Ash took careful aim, threw the ball as hard as he could, and missed.

"Sorry, chief. Better luck next time." The carny handed Ash a small mirror with a deformed-looking horse painted on it.

"What's this?" said Ash.

"It's your prize. Nice work, kid."

Ash practically went rigid. "But . . . wait a minute, I'm going to buy another try for the plane, O.K.?"

"No can do. Finito. No more chances. Though I *will* let you start over again, if you really want to." The carny made it sound as if he was being generous.

Ash's face turned radish red. "That's not fair!" he shouted. "You took all my money!"

"Hang on there, chief. You *gave* me all your money."

Ash threw the deformed-horse mirror in the dust and stamped on it. Shards of sparkling glass flew everywhere. It was so unlike him, I could hardly believe what I was seeing. Of course, I'd never seen Ash treated so unfairly.

"You cheater!" he yelled. "You cheated me! I don't even have anything left for the rides now!"

The carny rolled his eyes and shook his head. "Go tell it to your mommy. Now beat it before I call security."

Ash stumbled away from the booth with one arm over his eyes. He stood in the midway shaking with sobs, too stricken to move.

I pulled at his sleeve. "Hey, it's O.K. I've still got plenty of money. I'll lend you some for rides and stuff. It's not a big deal."

Ash pulled away from me, his eyes still hidden. I guess he wished I hadn't been there to witness his humiliation. Sometimes trying to be a good friend just makes things harder on people.

I felt the unner hanging like lead in my pocket. *Don't use it unless you have to,* the old man had said. Was it really me sending a message to myself?

But there was Ash, so mad and sad it made me want to cry right along with him. He was right—it wasn't fair. He deserved another chance at that airplane. But how important was it, in the big picture of things, for Ash to win? By now I knew there was just no way to tell. How was I supposed to know when I *had* to do something and when I only *wanted* to?

Ash hadn't asked me to use the unner, but I knew he must be thinking of it. I looked at him, hunched over as if somebody had punched him in the stomach. I had the power to help. What kind of a friend would stand there and do nothing?

I took the unner out of my pocket, turned it on,

and keyed in five minutes, just enough time for another try at the airplane. I closed my eyes and punched the red button.

Suddenly we were standing in front of the milk-bottle booth again. The carny said, "This is it, chief. Knock this one down and you get the plane."

Ash took careful aim . . . and missed again.

I unned another ninety seconds. Another miss. I frowned and made a deal with myself. I'd give it one more try. If he missed after three uns, I'd take it as a personal signal from the universe and give up.

Ash missed again. The universe had spoken.

Just as before, the carny said, "Sorry, chief. Better luck next time," and handed Ash the mirror with the horse on it.

"What's this?"

"It's your prize. Nice work, kid."

I felt like hiding my eyes as Ash said, "But . . . wait a minute, I'm going to buy another try for the plane, O.K.?"

I thought I knew what was coming next. But if there's one thing I know now, it's that the universe hardly ever does what you think it will. The carny should have said, "No can do." Instead, he sucked thoughtfully on his lower lip and looked at Ash as if sizing him up. I saw the moment when he made up his mind. "All right. One more chance. But only because I like you."

Ash dug in his pocket and came up with a quarter. He grimaced and looked at me. "Borrow twenty-five cents?" he said. "I'll pay you back tomorrow."

I gladly rummaged through my own pocket and came up with some coins. It seemed like a much safer and more honest way to help than using the unner had. I slapped the money into Ash's hand and said, "Blow 'em away!"

Ash threw the ball, and the milk bottles toppled with a clatter. A moment later, he practically danced across the midway with the airplane under his arm, while the carny frowned as if puzzled at himself.

"This is the best night of my life!" said Ash.

I nodded, hoping he was right, fearing he might be wrong. There was absolutely no way to predict how Ash's winning the plane might change things. Anything could happen now.

Suddenly, a dog trotted across the way in front of us. Not just any dog. *The mangy mutt.* I sucked my breath in sharply.

"What?" said Ash. "You look like you just saw a ghost."

"The dog! It's the one Roxy ran after—will run after—into the traffic."

Ash stopped and looked at me. "I just thought of something. Did this happen last time? I mean, did you know I was going to win the plane tonight?"

My stomach felt like there were worms squirming

around in it as I considered how to answer. "Yes. I mean, no. I mean, it didn't happen like this last time. Everything's already so different. Except that dumb dog. Why'd it have to be here?" I looked at my watch and felt even sicker. It was 8:15. I couldn't remember exactly when the accident would happen, but I knew the time was getting close.

"Cheer up!" said Ash. "Look, if it didn't happen like this last time, that's a great sign, right? It means maybe everything else will be different, too. So what if the dog's here? We haven't seen Roxy and Rainy. Maybe they decided not to come."

I glanced around. He was right. There was still no sign of them. I really, *really* wanted to believe that they hadn't come. But there were hundreds of people in the carnival crowd. Roxy and Rainy could easily be there somewhere, even if we hadn't seen them yet.

"I've got an idea," Ash continued. "Let's go on the Devil's Elevator. Once we're up there, we'll be able to see the whole park. If they're here, we'll spot them."

I thought it over. It was true that there was no better vantage point at the carnival. On the other hand, the last time I'd gone on that ride, I'd seen the world crash down around my shoulders. The idea of doing it again made me feel all scooped out somehow. I swallowed. It wasn't easy. "O.K., I guess so," I said in a small voice.

We made our way to the towering ride through

waves of strolling parents, excited children, and high-school couples holding hands. The air was thick with the mingled smells of dust, popcorn, and spilled soda pop. Ash picked out a woman behind the counter of a snack booth. She had dyed blond hair piled high on her head, dangly red earrings, and big gobs of green and purple eye shadow. But she smiled at people, and her smile looked real. He asked her to keep the airplane for him while we went on the ride, and she grinned, put one finger under his chin, and said, "Anything for you, cutie." Ash grinned back, and I thought I might get sick.

I handed over two tickets for the Devil's Elevator, and we stood in the line, which was short. I felt worse and worse as the minutes passed. Roxy had stood here, almost in this very spot, then run after the dog while I'd watched, helpless, in the metal cage above.

"Step inside, please." The gravelly voice of the ride operator jolted me out of my waking nightmare. He steadied the cage and held the door open for us.

Ash flung himself inside and buckled his seat belt. "Come on!" he called. "What're you waiting for?"

I stopped with one foot in the cage and one on the catwalk outside. "I . . . I've got a really bad feeling about this."

"Move it, will you?" said the carny, frowning. "People are waiting."

I stepped inside. My stomach was already spinning, and the ride hadn't even started yet. A too-small voice inside me squeaked, *Don't do this! Get out of here!* I told myself I was just being a chicken and an idiot and a baby. While I buckled my seat belt, the same group of four girls who'd been on the ride with us before climbed in, already screaming with excitement. I looked at Ash, and he rolled his eyes.

The cage jerked, grinding slowly upward. I grabbed the mesh with my fingers and stared through. Below us, the carnival seethed with moving bodies, lights, and colors. The music of the carousel floated up, rising and falling with the breeze. Maybe it was luck, who knows, but my gaze came to rest on the pony ride, and there was Lorraine lifting Roxy down from a little brown-and-white horse. I breathed easier when I saw that she was keeping a firm hold on Roxy's hand.

Roxy pointed at the snack booth and the kindly woman who was keeping Ash's plane for him. They walked toward it. Their voices were lost in the crowd and the wind, but I knew what they were talking about. Roxy would be asking for a candy apple, or Rainy would be suggesting it. The mangy dog ran past. Roxy gave a little leap of joy. Rainy let go of her hand to open her coin purse, and my heart went into warp speed.

Hardly anybody I know goes to church, except maybe a couple of times a year, on special holidays.

This includes my family. Ash's parents met in a spiritual commune in California, which is probably why Ash's name is Ashadha instead of something normal like Brian or even Julius. They never go to church at all. They just have a place in their house where they burn incense and practice "being mindful." Ash and I have talked about this before. The thing is, when we need to pray, neither of us ever knows who to pray to. Sometimes a person just wants to pray for something small, like not striking out or getting at least a C on a big test. But other times, you want to pray because you feel lost and you don't know what else to do. You want somebody bigger and more powerful than you are to be in charge. That's how I felt, watching Roxy tear off after that dog and knowing what would come next.

I pressed my face against the mesh and screamed, "Stop her! Stop her!" I don't know who I was pleading with. Anybody who might be listening, I guess.

Ash's breath brushed the back of my neck as he leaned close, watching from behind my shoulder without a word. He smelled like corn dogs and peanuts.

Lorraine whirled and looked around, suddenly aware that Roxy was gone. I heard her shout rise up thinly, "Roxy! Stop!" as she sped after my sister, her coin purse yawning and forgotten on the snack lady's counter.

I watched them dart through the carnival, the dog chased by Roxy chased by Lorraine, moving relentlessly closer to the street. I felt the line of heat from a tear trickling down my cheek. "Don't," I whispered. "Please, don't let it happen." Ash's breath stopped abruptly as the dog jumped off the curb. Lorraine was so close. She stretched hard, snatching at Roxy's sweater.

Somewhere in that moment before anything terrible had quite happened yet, I thought of using the unner—not waiting for the awful inevitable. But I was too late. The unner was only halfway out of my pocket when the dog ran in front of the truck. The driver stood on his brakes. I heard his tires squeal. Smoke rose from the pavement. Then the mysterious universe took over. Against all odds, Lorraine caught Roxy and spun her around, hurling her back to the sidewalk as if she'd been flung from the end of a crack-the-whip game. But Lorraine kept going in the opposite direction, unable to stop herself. The truck hit her and tossed her high, her body moving in ways that looked all wrong. I closed my eyes as the Devil's Elevator roared toward the ground. Only a few seconds had passed, but it seemed like forever.

By the time that stupid ride had stopped and the carny opened the cage door, I was crying hard, and I was so out of it I didn't care who saw. I stumbled down the ramp onto the midway, sobbing, the unner clutched in my hands. Ash sprinted ahead, dodging through the crowd toward the growing knot of gawkers in the street. He didn't look back. He probably assumed I was right behind him.

But my legs felt like overdone spaghetti. Instead of carrying me after Ash, they buckled, and I sat down hard in the dust. My throat opened and closed noisily as the sight of Lorraine spinning through the air replayed itself again and again in my head. This outcome was as bad as the first—maybe worse, because I felt doubly responsible for it. If I hadn't fooled around with fate, Rainy wouldn't even have been at the carnival. Even if she *was* annoying, I didn't want to see her hurt. I liked her. And I loved my sister. How could I choose which one of them would get hit by a truck? I had no clue. I thought I could change things for the better. But instead I'd messed them up more than ever. Now I saw the truth: I was like an ant trying to figure out rocket science. I was never going to get it. My brain just wasn't big enough. I grabbed a fistful of my hair and pulled. It hurt. I was so mad at myself and at the world, I pulled it again.

"Are you Gib?" said a voice from above. I looked up. Someone stood silhouetted in one of the brilliant lights along the midway.

I nodded, squinting, thinking maybe the old man from the woods had returned to help me. But though I couldn't see the face, I could tell the person's shape was wrong. I saw no wisps of silvery hair or tendrils of steam—just someone in a hood or a scarf. The voice, familiar but knobby as rough cloth, belonged to a woman.

A spidery finger reached out of the looming shadow and came to rest on the unner. The finger had an Egyptian scarab beetle tattooed on it.

Madam Isis!

"I have been visited by a messenger, an old man. Where he is from, who sent him, and why, I cannot tell you. All I will say is that he did not seem entirely of this world. He instructed me to find you and give you this message. You must have courage. Now is the time for action. Much hangs on this moment."

I gulped down a sob. "But what should I do?"

Madam Isis shook her head. "That is all he said."

Panic rose inside me, threatening to wash me away. I wished I could just sit in the dust and do nothing at all rather than risk doing the wrong thing again. *Now is the time for action. Much hangs on this moment.* The old man knew more about the big picture than anyone else, and he seemed to think anything at all was better than nothing. But why hadn't he just told me what to do? Maybe not even he knew.

I felt small and scared, trapped in a dark place I couldn't find my way out of. "Help me, Madam Isis! What should I do?" I cried, hiding my face in the crook of my arm.

I felt a gentle touch on my shoulder, and when I looked, I saw that the fortuneteller had knelt down beside me. "My friend," she said, "it is not so very hard. Look into your heart and do what you find there. For as long as I can remember, I have seen bits and pieces of what might lie ahead. And I can tell you this: what happens matters less than knowing you did your best. Only the heart knows what that may be."

She looked kind and wise. I believed her.

I tried to steady myself. I'd never felt so stupid before. Follow my heart? I couldn't even tell what my brain wanted, let alone my heart. Then it came to me.

There was one thing I wanted with every speck of me. I wanted Roxy and Rainy both to be all right. And there was only one possible way to get that: use the unner again.

How much more of this night could I stand to relive? As little as possible, I thought. I considered the various versions of reality through which I'd threaded my way. One thing was the same in all of them. The Devil's Elevator. Maybe if I didn't get on that ride, if I just stayed on the ground near Roxy, I could change everything. I could grab her hand and not let go, no matter what else happened. It wasn't much of a plan, but it had to be better than no plan at all.

I tried to estimate how much time had passed since Ash and I climbed into the Devil's Elevator—maybe fifteen minutes. I turned the unner on. Goose bumps rose on my arms as the machine made the little silver bell sound that meant it was ready. I punched MMODE and keyed in 15. I looked at Madam Isis, and she smiled. I pushed **ORDER**.

The world jerked, and I found myself standing in line again. I'd made the mistake of keeping my eyes open, and I was dizzy. I bumped into Ash.

"Whoa!" he said. "What's wrong?"

I blinked at him. His face glowed bright with eagerness and excitement. He was, after all, looking forward to a thrilling ride he'd never tried before.

"Nothing. I just . . . I just . . ." I figured I might as well tell him right then. "Ash, I can't go on this ride."

"What?" He looked as if I'd just told him I was growing a tail. "What's the matter?"

I rubbed my sleeve hastily across my eyes, still wet with tears. How much more embarrassing could life get? "Nothing," I said for the second time. "I can't go on this ride, that's all. You can go by yourself if you want. It's O.K."

"Are you out of your mind? We've been planning this for weeks! You have to go! It won't be any fun without you."

I shook my head. "Trust me. If I go, somebody's going to get hit by a truck."

For a minute, he didn't believe me. I could see his eyes moving as he tried to figure out what was going on, wondering if I'd turned chicken and was just using a lame excuse to get out of the ride. But at this point in the last version of time, he'd known about the unner; he'd even used it himself. He knew about Roxy and the accident that hadn't happened yet. I watched as he decided to trust me.

"You sure?" he said.

I nodded.

His shoulders and the corners of his mouth drooped. He wasn't very good at hiding disappointment. "Can we try again later?" he asked as he turned around to begin working his way out of the line.

"Maybe," I said, following him. *If there's a miracle,* I thought.

It was a tight squeeze. The line behind us was longer than it had been before, and there were a lot of people packed between the two metal guide rails leading up to the ride. It was hard for them to make space for us.

I accidentally stepped on a girl's foot. She shrieked. You'd have thought I was wearing jackboots with spikes in the soles—how much could an ordinary pair of canvas high tops hurt?

Then I saw her look up and bat her eyes at the guy she was with. He was big, and his T-shirt bulged with muscles, but I was so worried about Rainy and Roxy that somehow those facts didn't register right away. What *did* register was that she was faking to make it look as if I'd hurt her more than I really had. I've seen girls try to start fights between boys a number of times, and I have to say I just don't get it. What's the point? It makes me *really* mad, and this time was no exception.

I said the first thing that came into my head: "Cripes, don't have a cow."

The boyfriend turned toward me, his chunky face twisted in an angry scowl. "Watch it, shrimp!" he said, and he grabbed the front of my jacket, jerking me right off my feet.

People around us grumbled and squealed, upset at

being jostled. Ash turned around and said, "Hey! Leave my friend alone!"

"You want me to leave him alone? O.K." The guy sneered and threw me over the railing like a sack of potatoes. I somersaulted across the dirt and lay there gasping, all the wind knocked out of me.

"The unner!" I heard Ash cry.

Then there was another sound—the crunch of breaking plastic. I sat up just in time to see the unner spinning beneath the feet of people who didn't even notice they were kicking it, pieces spraying in all directions.

Ash squeezed under the railing and scurried into the crowd on his hands and knees like a mad mouse. He lunged toward what was left of the device, covering it with his body. Somebody stumbled over him. I heard him grunt. He got to his feet, shook himself off, and hurried over to help me up. He was still watching the ground in a stunned way as stray bits of the unner continued to ricochet from one person's feet to another's.

I spit out dirt as Ash handed me the mass of unidentifiable parts and dangling connectors. "This can't be happening," I said, staring at it, unwilling to believe my own eyes.

"Sorry," said Ash. "I tried to get it. I really did." He looked almost as desperate as I felt. "What now?"

"Now?" I said. I felt half dead inside, almost the

way I had in our Roxyless house after the first accident. It was hard to think or even feel. Nothing seemed real anymore. But I guess some part of me knew what was going on, and that part took over, urging me forward into my last chance of saving the world as I knew it.

I looked across the midway toward the pony ride and there, just as before, stood Roxy and Rainy, hand in hand. In my dazed state, they seemed as joyful and radiant as a pair of angels outlined in carnival lights. I'd rather have croaked right there than watch anything bad happen to either one of them. They walked toward the booth where the blond woman hawked her candy apples.

"Can I please, please have one?" said Roxy. "I love candy apples!"

"Sure," said Rainy, smiling. She stroked Roxy's hair.

I walked over to them, trying a smile of my own. "Pretty hard to eat those without front teeth," I said.

Lorraine looked up. "Oh, Gib! Ash! Hi," she said. She started to grin but stopped halfway, probably remembering how rude I'd been when I left the house.

Roxy stuck her tongue out at me and said, "Doesn't matter. I can so eat it without my front teeth." Then she looked at me hard. "Eeeuuw! What happened to *you?*"

I looked down at myself. I was filthy. Pale dust caked my shirt and jacket, and unidentifiable carnival gunk was stuck to my jeans. I didn't even want to know what my face looked like. The tip of my nose felt funny, and when I reached up to touch it, my finger came away red. I'd scraped it in exactly the same place as I had when I tripped in the woods an eternity ago.

"Gosh, Gib, what did happen to you? You look like you've been in a fight," said Lorraine. Worry lines dented her forehead, and I thought, *Maybe she doesn't hate me. Not deeply, anyway.*

I smiled. "Oh, I'm O.K. I mean, it wasn't exactly a fight. Just kind of. No big deal." I looked down at Roxy. "How about that candy apple?" I said. I took her hand, the one Lorraine wasn't holding. I thought Roxy might object, but instead she was happy.

"Yaaaay! You guys can swing me!" she said, lifting her feet off the ground, practically tearing our arms out of their sockets. Rainy and I rolled our eyes at each other at the exact same time, then laughed as we swung Roxy toward the snack booth.

From the corner of my eye, I saw the mangy stray dog running our way. I thought maybe I could distract Roxy, so I said, "Hey, Rox, want to see a trick I learned?"

She put her feet back on the ground and looked at me with suspicion. "What kind of trick? Is it a mean one?"

"Would I play a mean trick on you?"

She frowned, unconvinced, and I knew why. *Of course* I would play a mean trick on her. I'd certainly done it enough times in the past.

But now the only thing that mattered was keeping her distracted, whether she believed me or not, so I tried frantically to think up a trick, any trick. I spotted a box of paper-wrapped soda straws on the counter beside the mustard. "Watch this!" I tugged her toward the counter so I could reach a straw with one hand while holding on to her with the other. I bit the end of the paper off and began to inch it down the straw, thinking I'd show her how to blow into one end and shoot the paper off the other like an arrow. It didn't have to be a great trick, after all, just a distracting one.

"Two candy apples, please," said Lorraine, and she dropped Roxy's hand so she could open her coin purse. But I still held the other hand and I tightened my grip just for good measure.

"Hey, that hurts!" Roxy yelled.

Instinctively, I relaxed my hand a little. Roxy sensed it and slipped free, glaring at me and rubbing her wrist as if I'd mortally wounded her. I dropped the straw and reached to grab hold of her again, but she dodged. She was fast. It was like trying to catch a bird.

The dog ran right between us, panting and wild-eyed, his fur brushing our shins. Now that I saw him up close, he looked lost and confused, and I was glad

I'd stopped myself from hitting him with rocks in front of our house.

"Oh, poor doggy! You need help!" cried Roxy, grinning like a maniac. Before I could stop her, she was gone.

I ran after her, dodging mothers with strollers and bumping into people. Everything I saw was clouded by despair, and I thought that maybe some events were small, like pebbles in a river. You could pick them up and toss them away without much trouble. But other events were like boulders that stuck up high and were so huge and heavy that the water of time changed course to flow around them, and they were nearly impossible to move. Maybe this moment was just too massive to erase. Maybe the best I could hope for was to shift it ever so slightly.

Thanks to the unner, there were now three of us trying to move that boulder—though Rainy didn't know that's what she was doing. She and Ash and I sped through the carnival like crazy heroes in a comic book no one's ever heard of.

"Stop that little girl!" Ash yelled, turning heads as he ran past. But nobody moved to help us.

"Roxy, stop!" Lorraine cried, a few steps behind him.

"Stop, Roxy!" I shrieked. But she ran on as if she hadn't heard. Not knowing what else to do, I shouted at the dog. "Stop, you doofus mutt!"

The dog turned and looked at me for about half a second, then took off again.

By the time we reached the curb, Roxy was almost on top of the dog, I was almost on top of her, and Ash and Lorraine were almost on top of me. Ash and Rainy lunged toward Roxy and the dog at the same time. I remember thinking I couldn't let it happen; we were all going to end up dead in the street unless I stopped us somehow. With one last, desperate push, I leaped harder and farther than any of the others. Ash, Rainy, Roxy, and the dog piled into me, pushing me over the curb. I thought, as I watched the wheels of the truck spin toward me, that even if it wasn't the best possible ending, it was all right. Better me than my sister or my friends.

MY THOUGHTS
ABOUT THE
UNIVERSE

You know I didn't die—otherwise I wouldn't be telling this story. I can't remember much about what happened next, but Ash and Rainy told me later that I did a somersault into the street, the truck flying toward me, its tires smoking like something straight from the underworld. It almost stopped in time.

Which is how I happen to be telling you this story while lying here on a cot under the autumn stars, suffering nothing worse than a badly broken leg. Some people think it's terribly unfair, what happened to me, like a punishment I don't deserve. "Poor Gib," I heard one of our neighbors say to another when she thought no one else was listening. "It's so awful. All that pain, all those surgeries, and even so he'll never be able to run with the other kids again." Others, including my parents, think I'm a hero because I kept Ash and Roxy and Rainy from ending up under the truck, too. They see it as bravery and incredible luck.

But I wasn't feeling brave at the time; in fact, I was scared out of my mind. I'm not very comfortable talking about luck anymore. And I'm not sure I ever really believed bad things happen because people deserve them. I definitely don't believe that now. I think it's something else—something more like balance, or lessons we need to learn but can't any other way. Which is kind of spooky, too, because if things happen so we can learn stuff from them, that means there must be a Big Teacher out there somewhere, thinking up Major Lesson Plans. I did learn something, though it's awfully hard to put it into words. And I know I made some kind of bargain so things would turn out the way they did; I'm just not sure what it is yet.

I have a few clues, though.

The doctor says I'll probably have a bad limp for the rest of my life, which pretty much answers the main question about the old guy in the woods—the stranger who knew way more than he possibly could have about my private life and who walked with a very bad limp. Ash was right. He had to be me. Funny how you're always the last person to recognize yourself.

My mom signed up for a high-tech grocery delivery service, and they gave her a special little terminal to plug into our home computer. Something about it seemed familiar, and when I looked closely, I saw what it was. It had a big red button that said **ORDER**. I opened the cigar box where I've been keeping the remains of the unner and discovered the order button was missing. But now I know where to find it when the time comes.

The thing that totally convinced me of Old Gib's true identity, though, was the dog. Roxy refused to let go of that crazy stray, even after the paramedics had rushed me away and Ash and Rainy and the policemen were left trying to figure out what to do with her. So the dog came to live at our house—temporarily, of course. Mom and Dad put an ad in the newspaper describing it and asking its owners to phone. But nobody ever called. Roxy was ecstatic, because the deal was that if we didn't get an answer within two weeks, she could keep the dog.

"I can name him now, right?" she said yesterday, clasping her hands together, jumping up and down. I smiled at her, thinking that I'd never, ever have to play doggy again.

Dad said yes, she could give the dog a name. He and Mom had been strict about it, insisting that we couldn't name him until we were sure he was ours. So we'd just been calling him "mutt" or "dog" or "boy."

Roxy stared at him so hard she actually held still for maybe two seconds. Then she shouted, "I've got it! I know his name! Doofus!"

Mom frowned and said, "Roxy, that's not very nice. How would you like to be called Doofus?"

Roxy pursed her lips and lifted her nose. "I'd be proud to be named Doofus, considering."

"Considering what?" said Mom.

"Gib called him Doofus Mutt when we were all chasing him, and it must have been the right name, because Doofus stopped and looked right at Gib. He really did. No fooling!"

"Doofus?" said Dad.

"Doofus," said Mom.

They looked at each other and shook their heads. But I was grinning, because I finally understood why the old man had asked how Doofus was. We had no dog named Doofus yet, but he knew there was one waiting in our near future. And judging from the way he asked, Doofus mattered as much to him as he already does to me.

The only reasonable conclusion is that I have a busy and exciting life ahead. Think about it: I'm going to have to invent both the unner and some method of time travel that'll make it possible for me to deliver it to my younger self. And when I do, I'm going to be in a hurry. Otherwise, why would I forget the zero, and why would I always have to leave myself in the woods too soon? The really big question is why I would be in a hurry. If I can travel in time, then I should have all the time in the world. It gives me the shivers to think about it, but there's only one answer. I keep remembering how slowly Old Gib moved, and how easily he got tired. I must be so old that I'm dying when I solve the problem of time travel. It makes me want to get started right away.

I've still got plenty of unanswered questions. I wish I knew exactly what Old Gib meant when he said I'm important in the world, and so is Roxy. I'm guessing that at some point in the future, Roxy and I will do some big or little thing that makes a bunch of other things happen. And in the end, whatever those things are, they're important in some mysterious way we won't understand till we get there.

All I know for sure, though, is that sometimes what seems bad is actually not so bad after all, and what seems good might not be when you see the big picture. Maybe bad things happen because without them we couldn't recognize good things. Maybe there's some law like conservation of motion, and for every good thing there has to be an equal and opposite bad thing. Take Ash winning that plane, for example. The day after the carnival, he took it over to the park, started it up, and flew it straight into a tree. Turns out it was a piece of junk, and the controls didn't work. Ultimately, winning it made him just as mad and disappointed as not winning it. But then who knows which of us would have wound up under the truck if I hadn't used the unner to help him win. There's just no way to tell.

It's all incredibly complicated. I've been lying here worrying a lot about whether I messed things up royally by first inventing and then using the unner. Suppose there really is Somebody in charge—Somebody who has, or had, a perfectly balanced Plan. Did my using the unner change it? Or was the unner part of the Plan in the first place? I hope, in the end, unning what happened to Roxy was for the best, because it'll be a long time before I know for sure, if I ever do, and even longer before I have the Power of Un again. If Madam Isis were here, I'd ask her if I did the right thing. But she isn't, and maybe it's just as well. Even if she knows bits and pieces of the future, how could she answer a question like that? How could anybody?

Nobody's out here now except me and the stars and Doofus scratching a flea. But I think I hear Ash's voice in the house, and maybe Rainy's, too. They said they'd come over tonight so we could watch some movies together.

I hope we choose the right ones.

Nancy Etchemendy lives in the San Francisco Bay area with her husband, John, and their son, Max. She's the author of several science-fiction books for children, and her writing earned her a Bram Stoker Award in 1999.

The Power of Un won the Bram Stoker Award in 2000 and was named an honor book by the Charles A. and Anne Morrow Lindbergh Foundation.